THEM

Copyright @ Mique Watson

14/05/23

ISBN: 9798394637582

Imprint: Independently Published

All Rights Reserved

Printed in the USA

Cover and wrap design by Grim Poppy

Editing and formatting by Judith Sonnet

The events, characters, and locations in this book are all fictional. Any resemblance to reality is unintended and coincidental.

No part of this book may be reprinted or transcribed without the author's written permission.

THEM: An Extreme Horror Novella

WARNING: This is an extreme horror novella. It features graphic, disturbing, and offensive content. It is not recommended to sensitive readers, or readers under the age of 18.

THEM

"The earth is evil. We don't need to grieve for it." (Melancholia, 2011. Dir. Lars von Trier)

THEM

An Extreme Horror Novella

By

Mique Watson

THEM

WARNING
THIS IS EXTREME HORROR
IT IS DISTURBING, DARK, TWISTED,
OFFENSIVE... AND FUCKED UP!

READ AT YOUR OWN RISK, CUNT-FACE!

THEM
CHAPTER 1

The soothing thunder rumbled outside. It was close to spring, and the promise of oncoming rain settled over her like a gentle breeze. Jeanette Wilson was parked on the couch, decompressing after a long day at work. She nursed a tall glass of Prosecco as the news played on the TV as background noise. She'd worked as a telemarketer and had to talk to people all day.

Jeanette had lived alone for three years now and had just got out of a long-term relationship. If it had taught her anything, it was that relationships weren't her *thing*. She was an introvert who spent her time trying to sell software to old white people via cold calls. She was verbally abused on the phones all day and didn't have the emotional bandwidth to spare on anyone—let alone romance. The only love she had in her heart was for her blonde Labrador, Nico.

The rain came down harder. The long week at work had flattened her. Despite having the morning shift, she'd been asked to do some over-time. Rent in Texas had gone up since the recession, and groceries had gotten more expensive.

She rued the day she'd taken the job—but no one else was hiring; this was the best she could do. She'd

THEM

applied for jobs high and low, and eventually settled on the first one that hired her. She had a dog to feed, after all. She'd never seen Nico as a burden. Every time she was down, all she had to do was run her hand through his velvety fur–the sudden spark of affection in his eyes filled her heart to the brim.

Her stomach grumbled, prompting her to look at the wall clock. It read 9:02pm. Where had the time gone? She wouldn't normally eat this late, but the cool, rainy weather had a calming effect on her. All she wanted to do was curl up on the blanket next to Nico and drift off into an easy, rejuvenating sleep knowing she had nothing going on the next day. Everything was perfect as it was: the grueling week had ended, she wasn't expected anywhere tomorrow, and she knew she wouldn't have to wake up to the obnoxious alarm that plagued her every morning.

Her stomach growled at her once again.

Cursing under her breath, she ambled toward the refrigerator and opened the door. Her eyes immediately landed on the extra tray of sushi she'd taken home yesterday in anticipation of how exhausted she'd be to cook today. *Thank you, past Jeanette.* She thought to herself. It was a Salmon Aburi with a side of pickled radish, wasabi, and Japanese mayonnaise. She

THEM

set it on the kitchen island and poured herself another glass of prosecco.

She survived on a diet of takeout, processed food, and pre-made meals from the grocery. The anxiety that had come with this job caused her to gain about forty pounds since she'd started with the company.

The woman who stared back at her in the kitchen mirror was in a decrepit state. The pasty white skin of her face was framed by her stringy, strawberry blonde hair. Her demeanor was dull, and her smiles were forced. She was so exhausted she felt like her skin was coated in a flaxen aura of grime.

Something peculiar came from the TV. She took her food to the couch to turn up the volume.

"... So far twenty people have been reported murdered in gruesome ways in the past two days. Every case has suggested that there were no signs of a break-in. The victims were likely killed by people they knew.

"What the fuck?" Jeanette whispered under her breath.

"...all these attacks took place in the victims' houses. We advise everyone to stay vigilant as authorities continue their efforts in investigating these unusual circum–"

She flipped the channel to HBO. She'd just finished

THEM

the most stressful week at work since she started at the company, and she wasn't going to let her evening be ruined by bad news.

She'd just lost her appetite.

Jeanette knew that the news was sensationalized—if it bleeds, it leads!-yet, she couldn't help but listen to that insidious voice at the back of her head. The voice that told her that *it could happen to you too*. This voice played over and over in a vicious loop, like a starving python coiled around her neck. Her chest constricted, her breath grew short and rapid—she forced herself to take a deep inhale in a futile effort to calm down.

She recalled the advice her father had given her; breathe in for seven seconds, hold your breath for five, and exhale for ten. She deployed his advice with precision, chiding her bothered mind.

After a few repetitions of the breathwork, her heart rate subsided, and she managed to focus on the TV. Stanley Kubrick's adaptation of *The Shining* was played on HBO. She'd always loved it, in spite of its differences from the book. She had found it amusing how she loved the book and the film despite how Stephen King detested that adaptation. At the end of the day, it was Kubrick—and Kubrick on his worst day was still better than almost every other director out there.

THEM

Horror flicks always soothed her–they reminded her of her father. Her father let her watch her first scary movie, *Invasion of the Body Snatchers*, when she was just eleven. It had terrified her so much she couldn't sleep without a night light for months. There was no denying that it had had a lasting effect on her; the thrill of it had been something she'd sought out again and again. It had become a ritual between the two of them; something they enjoyed together to cope with the stresses of the world. She scooched closer to Nico now that she'd settled on what to do: she'd watch *The Shining*, she'd eat her sushi, she'd finish her glass of wine, and then she'd go to bed.

A loud ruckus jolted her out of her seat. It came from her phone. Storms were common where she lived at this time of year; sure enough, on the screen there was a weather alert. Looking outside, it seemed about right.

The thunder grumbled even louder, and she had to turn the volume of the TV up to max just to hear what Jack Nicholson was saying. It was the iconic scene where he chased Wendy into her room. She locked herself in the bathroom. The lock jangled as Jack tried to jimmy it open, and then the ax descended on the

THEM

white door. Again, and again. The scene made Jeanette's heart jump, even though she'd already seen the film in its entirety about fifteen times—it still has the same startling effect on her.

And now Jack Torrance was about to deliver the iconic line...

"Here's Joh..."

The screen cut to black.

A wave of static boomed out from the TV's speaker.

Nico unleashed a fit of barks as she hurriedly turned the volume down. As she patted him down, a blocky neon text flashed on the television.

EMERGENCY BROADCAST.

A blanket of silence descended over everything.

She scanned the room and her attention stopped at the clock. It read 10pm. She hadn't even touched her dinner. She flipped the channel, but every channel cut to that same silent broadcast. She picked up a roll of sushi with her chopsticks, but as she brought it to her mouth her hands shook uncontrollably. She breathed in for seven seconds, but nothing eased the sense of impending doom. She put the food down and picked up her phone, dialing her support system. He picked it up after the first ring.

"Dad?"

THEM

"Hey Jen, is everything alright?"

"Y-yeah," she noticed a slight quiver in her voice, "I was just watching a movie and I got this weird broadcast... it seems to be on every channel."

"We seem to have that same problem too. Janice and I were watching this lifetime movie and it cut out at the best part! Would you believe it? They were just about to reveal who the..."

Static.

"Dad?"

"T—g—ww..."

Static.

"Dad!"

"S—, Honey, the line is c—g o..."

The call abruptly ended.

She dialled again, but the call wasn't going through. Service was shoddy where she lived, though it was never *this* bad. Her dad had even offered to house her until she could get on her feet, but she had refused. As much as she loved him, she couldn't help but feel like an emotionally needy burden.

Her mother had passed away from liver failure when she was a kid, and her dad had since remarried. She loved Janice, but most of all loved seeing her father happy again. The last thing she wanted to do was get in

THEM

the way of his happiness, so she sucked it up and moved to this small, seemingly deserted town despite her dad disapproving of the location. Cheap rent and semi-stable income came at a price.

The anxiety slowly crept in.

Jeanette knew that everyone in the general area was likely watching the same broadcast, but she couldn't help but feel like the broadcast targeted her and her alone. Not having the control to run away from it unnerved her; she felt a looming sense of danger with her name on it.

Someone started speaking.

"This is an emergency broadcast system from the state of Texas. We request that all residents lock up for the night until further notice. Do not open the door for *anyone...* We— a—-.. T—t, y—...."

Static.

Static.

Static.

"... they look like people."

The sudden explosion of a fuse box from the distance startled Jeanette.

It was a concussive noise, which reminded Jeanette of a champagne bottle being popped across the room. Everything went dark. The power had gone out, and

THEM

Nico erupted into another fit of barks. Outside the window, all the houses on the street started going dark, one after the other, like falling dominoes.

"Nico, easy boy!"

Nico huddled into her like a scared child.

Everything was dark.

She raced to the curtain, slightly slipping on some socks on the floor. She inched closer to the window and opened the blinds, but there was no moonlight. *What happened?* She thought before she was seized by a cold blast of wind.

She took out her phone in an attempt to turn on the flashlight. Before she could unlock the device, her eyes had somewhat adjusted to the darkness. A figure cloaked in black stood in the window across the room. Her shallow breathing and rapidly increasing heart rate made the specter loom in and out of focus.

Finally, she unlocked her phone and switched on the flashlight. When she flashed the light in front of her, her blood froze. The humanoid shape wasn't looking at her from a window–because it wasn't a window; it was a mirror.

Panicking, she swiped up her contact list and stabbed at her dad's name. Her teeth chattered, and her mind raced a thousand miles a minute. The phone rang...

THEM

... and rang.

... and rang.

Jeanette killed the call and dialed again, but the result was the same: it just rang out.

"Fuck. Shit." She spat, exasperated.

A knock at the door sent a chill down her spine.

She stopped to rationalize the situation in her head. *Maybe there must be a mistake? Who would be out in a storm? But the storm had subsided. Maybe it was her neighbor, Anna, a middle-aged woman who lived by herself and needed some company,* she thought.

Anna had likely sauntered over with an umbrella now that the storm had subsided. It was still raining, but the rain wasn't as intense as it was before the announcement.

The thought of having some human company to wait out the night with her was calming, but she still had to double check. She crept over to the window to see who it was. Pulling the curtain back, she saw the shape of someone by the door. She flashed her phone flashlight at it to get a better look.

It wasn't Anna.

THEM
CHAPTER 2

She was smitten by this man at her workplace named Brandon. He was in a different department—but the two had met at a company function and instantly hit it off. She'd been charmed by his friendliness and affectionate demeanor; he was an extrovert who occasionally brought out her latent social butterfly.

The only problem was he was twenty years her senior and married. Another issue was, she had slept with him several times. They'd met at bars and hotels. He had confided in her about some problems in his marriage but maintained that he had no plans on leaving his wife. She was fully aware of this the first time they made love. After the sex, guilt instantly ate her up from the inside. Even when she told herself that this was his fault—that they were on their own separate journey, the shame hadn't subsided.

And now he was standing by her door.

What the hell is he doing here?

He'd never show up unannounced—heck, she couldn't even recall telling him her address. Something queer lingered in the back of her mind. She couldn't quite put her finger on it.

Brandon's gaze was firmly locked on hers.

THEM

He stood still, smiling. Except the smile had a bizarre quality to it—he was completely frozen in a grin that seemed to be a rehearsed parody of what a smile ought to look like. About a minute had passed, and he hadn't even blinked; he was still smiling with that strained expression. His eyes were completely expressionless, but his mouth pinched with how wide the grin was.

She waved at him, but he just stood there. It was an uncanny valley that sent shockwaves through her system. He hadn't just stopped—he had stopped mid breath. His chest didn't rise and fall. He stood still, as if it were a scene in a movie that had been paused.

She walked around to her front door and squinted into the peephole.

Darkness.

A flash of lighting cracked in the sky for a second, and at that moment she saw that he made direct eye contact with her through the peephole with that disturbed smile.

Just a glimpse sent a chill through her.

"Brandon?" Her voice caught in her throat.

Behind her, Nico growled. He'd always been a good-natured dog; this behavior was very much out of character. Flashing the light on him, she could see his skin was bunched up between his eyes, his tail was still,

THEM

and jaw was clenched. He trembled with distress and anger.

Brandon started banging on the door, hammering it with his fists. Nico erupted, once again, in a fit of barks.

Brandon's knocking became more aggressive.

She returned to the window to see him, but the sight of him grew even murkier in the darkness.

She hastily directed her attention elsewhere. In the house across the street, Anna sat in her candle-lit living room with a book. Jeanette tried to get her attention by waving the phone, but the desperate signal went unnoticed. She quickly dialed her number. After a few rings, Anna turned and left the room. She was now completely out of sight.

No. no. no.

The loud knocking stopped.

Everything came to a standstill.

Nico still stood by the door, glaring at it in the darkness. His growling was intermittent, but the barking had stopped. The phone continued to ring until,

"Jeanette, hi."

She practically jumped out of her skin at the sudden sound of someone speaking. She quickly realized that

THEM

Anna had likely left the room to search for her phone.

"H-hello... It's me."

"Are you alright dear? I can practically hear your teeth chattering over the phone line."

"I-I'm alright. I'm sorry, I just needed to ask... I just..."

What did she need to ask? She had entered the situation with no gameplan–it wasn't enough to just hear someone's voice, although the sound of another human did comfort her. She didn't know what to say, all she knew was that she wanted to prolong the conversation as long as she possibly could. She recalled a conversation she had had with Anna the other day about her Apple Strudel recipe. No, she couldn't bring that up out of nowhere. It was the middle of a storm, and it wouldn't make sense–she couldn't bake in the darkness. Maybe she could say that she was calling Anna back? But as far as she remembered, the two had rarely ever spoken on the phone. They had the kind of relationship where, if someone ran out of sugar, they'd just show up unannounced. Her mind pinballed in all directions, desperately groping for something to say.

"Jeanette, are you still there? What do you need?"

Impatience laced Anna's tone. Jeanette gripped the phone in her hand, desperately searching for

THEM

something to say. She decided to just go with the obvious.

"I-I was just checking in to see how you were doing with the storm and all..."

"Oh, yes the lights went off. Luckily, I have a stockroom with candles. It was a challenge to navigate my house in the dark at first, but I know the place like the back of my hand," she let out a soft chuckle, "we used to get storms and blackouts here all the time! Having a stash of candles has always been a force of habit, you see..."

Anna prattled on. She usually got like this when they'd spend time together over afternoon tea. Anna was shy at first, giving her one-word answers, only asking closed questions. Jeanette wasn't an extrovert, so the ins and outs of human interaction were lost on her. What she did know was that once Anna found something to talk about, she wouldn't give up. Even the smallest personal anecdote could be spoken about by her for hours. Brevity wasn't Anna's strong suit, and these long-winded tangents normally annoyed Jeanette.

Something was off.

Nico!

The eerie lack of his barking sent shivers down her

THEM

spine. She reached down, only to feel air. She could've sworn Nico was sitting right next to her; he was just at her feet a minute ago.

"Hey, Anna," she said, cutting her neighbor off mid-sentence.

"Yes dear, is something the matter?"

"Sorry, I didn't mean to cut you off. I was just spooked because there's a man outside my house, and I wasn't expecting him."

"Oh, is he someone you know?"

The guilt of the affair started to bubble up in her again.

"Y-yes, but not that well. I don't know, he was just being kind of aggressive, and it spooked me."

Jeanette's spine felt like it could crawl out of her body.

Three houses far down the block still had their power. *Why was it just those ones, weren't we all on the same grid? They probably have a generator.* She contemplated this.

Then a flash.

The furthest house lights went out. All of them at the same time.

Jeanette cursed herself for not knowing the mobile numbers of her other neighbors. Her anti-social

THEM

behavior hadn't ever been this much of a hindrance.

A sharp glance to the right showed her that Brandon was no longer there. Could he see her? Was he watching her in the distance? She let out a sigh, telling herself that this was all in her head; that, any moment now, the power would go on and her pleasant evening would resume.

"Jen, are you still there?"

She switched on the phone flashlight and turned around, "Yeah, sorry, my dog is just..."

"Jeanette?"

She sucked in a sharp breath. The pale hue of a man stood in the line of her phone flashlight. The off-white glow bounced off his sickly pale skin making it look like a mugshot of him stood in front of her.

"You... how did you get in?"

He paused, regarding her like she was crazy. His eyes were vacant when they should've been inquisitive.

"What's wrong? It's me."

"Yes, I can see that. How did you get in?"

"The back door was unlocked so I just walked in. What's gotten into you? You look like you've seen a ghost. Look, let me just..."

Brandon started walking toward her.

"No! Stay there."

THEM

"What? Jeanette. Baby, listen."

Baby? Since when did he refer to me as baby? His pet name for her was Jen. Occasionally he'd call her *hun*. Jeanette clearly tried to convey that she was uncomfortable with the whole situation–yet he remained staunchly unperturbed.

"You've never shown up here unannounced before–why are you here, Brandon?"

"I just wanted to see you. Is that not good enough? Am I not good enough?"

No. It fucking isn't. Who does he think he is? Their relationship was purely sexual and nothing else–the brazenness this man displayed vexed her. She had to think of something–something quick. She elects to play dumb–to use his own sordid tactics against him.

"Sorry, I've just been on edge. I haven't been sleeping all that well, and with all this shit happening... I'm just not in the best headspace."

His facial expression hadn't shifted a single time–the only way she'd been able to detect his emotion was through the inflection of his voice.

"It's alright, baby. I get it."

Baby. There it fucking is again.

This was certainly not the man she'd been fucking all this time. The Brandon she knew respected her

THEM

boundaries. *Could he have been a crazy stalker who is now going to murder me in a crime of passion like the kind I'd see on Dateline and Sixty Minutes?* She had to figure out if it was really him once and for all. She couldn't alert him to her suspicions, though. She had to be indirect in her inquest.

"Come, let's sit on the couch. I'm tired."

"Great idea!" he said.

Not a single shift in his facial muscles registered, however. It was the eeriest thing.

He sat down next to her. The entire time, his eyes were firmly locked on hers, yet she still tried to play it cool. She was worried that he'd read too much into her action (or inaction).

"So, how's life been?" she started.

"It's been fine. Thank you for asking. And you?"

"Not too bad. It was a really grueling week, but I'm glad it's over. Before the blackout happened, Nico and I were just watching a movie."

"Oh, which movie?"

"*The Shining*. Have you seen it?"

"No," he chuckled uneasily, "can't say I have."

Except he has.

One night, over a romantic candle-lit dinner, she'd told him about her relationship with her father and

THEM

how much she loved this film. Brandon must've spent about fifteen straight minutes animatedly professing his love for Stanley Kubrick. Hearing him be as passionate as he was about Kubrick's oeuvre was part of what endeared her to him in the first place! She'd learned more about *A Clockwork Orange*'s subliminal messages from him than she ever did looking the film up herself. It's his favorite Kubrick—no, his favorite film.

"Oh, well maybe you should check it out one day," she said, feigning blitheness, "what's your favorite movie, then?"

He sat silently for a moment. "I wouldn't know. I'm not much of a film buff. I'd love to hear some of your recommendations, though."

Except he is a fucking film buff! she thought. Bells and whistles clanged in her head.

"Sure. Anyway, so how are Anna and the kids."

"Oh, right. They're fantastic. They're doing perfectly well if I do say so myself."

"So the pregnancy hasn't been too much of a hassle, then?"

"No, not at all!"

"That's great to hear, Brandon. Really. " She forced a smile and gave him a gentle, consoling rub on the

THEM

shoulder.

Except none of this was *great* to hear at all. His wife's name wasn't Anna—it was Rayna. And she's never been pregnant. One of the reasons he was so frustrated was because she was infertile. Almost every time they slept together he'd complain about how exasperated he was that she didn't want kids as much as he did despite them agreeing to have them. He'd rant and rave about how little effort she was putting into researching other methods like IVF and surrogacy. Part of the reason, she recalled, that he'd even initiated the affair was to somehow get back at his unapologetically apathetic wife.

Whoever this was, it was *not* Brandon.

Her instincts told her this the second she laid eyes on him, but now it—whatever it was—had practically outright admitted to it to her. She postulated more solutions in her head. Just then, the sound of her phone ringing interrupted her train of thought.

"Sorry, I've got to get this," She said.

He nodded. She got up and walked to the bathroom, locking herself in. She exhaled a sigh and let her back slump against the wooden surface of the door. She slouched and brought the phone up to her head.

"Hey, sorry, I..."

THEM

The sound of footsteps fell right behind the door. The uneasiness slithered up her spine like a venomous snake poised to strike at any moment.

"Jeanette! It's Anna... something is wrong. There's something scratching on my door," she said, sounding distressed.

Jeanette rolled her eyes–she didn't have time to deal with this of all things now.

"It's probably just a raccoon."

"It's not a raccoon. It's at my back door. I think it's a man! He's..." Anna's voice sounded like that of a child who had just found the boogeyman in her closet. The effect was extremely disconcerting.

"What?" Jeanette interrupted.

"He's... oh, Frank, what are you doing outs—"

"Anna, what's going on?"

"Oh, it's Frank. I don't know what he's up to... Frank, what are you doing outside? Come back in at once before–"

A scream pierced Jeanette's ear.

She pulled the device away from her as the loud, piercing shriek assaulted her. The frantic sound was audible even as she held the phone away from her head. Electric currents shredded through her muscle fiber. A fissure tore through the fabric of her once

THEM

tranquil, predictable existence.

"Anna? Anna?!"

No one answered.

The call had been disconnected.

In a moment of panic, she recalled the advice her father had given her when she couldn't sleep at night. He'd sit at the foot of her bed and gently guide her through the breathwork. He'd then ask her the same question he did every time she was inconsolable: "What do we do when we're scared, Jennie bug?"

"We tell ourselves that we are bigger than our fear and that we will keep on living no matter what. The fear is passing, it will eventually end..." she whispered to herself, clutching the phone to her chest.

She breathed in. At the top of the breath she counted to seven, and then let out a long exhale. She repeated this several times, and then unlocked her phone. She reduced the volume, hit redial, and brought the phone back to her head.

Ring.

Ring.

Ring.

Ring.

Ring.

"The number you've dialed is unavailable. Please try

THEM

again later. The number you d—"

Damn it.

Jeanette looked back at Anna's house. The candle had been snuffed out. The entire street was now cloaked in pitch black darkness.

The rain grew stronger.

She strained to hear the potential struggle happening behind Anna's walls, but the impenetrable downpour stifled her efforts. The only light was the glow on her phone screen.

And then her phone rang.

All the breathwork had been for naught; her heart-rate beat a million miles a minute once more. The name Anna was on the screen. She immediately picked the call up,

"Anna? What the fuck is going on?"

"Jeanette..." She spoke in hushed tones, but it was clear that she was sobbing, "Frank is..." she choked back a sob, "Frank is..."

"Frank is... what?" Jeanette snapped.

"He's dead, Jen, he's dead... oh god," it sounded like it took everything in her to not break out into a full wail, "please, come help."

Frank? Dead? How? All of this was happening at once; a million thoughts ran through her head.

THEM

"W-what?"

"Please let me in," Brandon said outside the door.

"Brandon, I'm on the phone... Give me a second."

"Jen..." Anna's voice shook, "please tell me you didn't let anyone in your house..."

What else could she say? She did. And she wasn't entirely sure if it was someone, or *something*. Anna went silent. Rattling, raspy breathing bellowed up and down behind the door.

The doorknob started to shake violently.

"Brandon, I said give me a fucking minute!"

"He's in the house with you? No... Jen..."

"Let me in!" Brandon yelled.

The rap turned into a furious series of pounds. The door shook and hit Jeanette's back. She pressed her back on the door, praying that it would hold still–willing god or the universe to keep the damned thing on its hinges as this madman struck blow after blow.

The assault eventually stopped.

"Baby..." his voice quivered in a shrill lilt.

The whimper turned to sobs–the heavy mewls seethed out of him with boiling indignation. His sobs then morphed into a sick, demented cackle. It was inhuman. It was the screaming noise of a pig being led to slaughter. The laughing pierced through the door

THEM

and reverberated throughout the walls.

And all at once, just as soon as it started—it stopped.

Silence.

The rain began to calm.

The cackle dimmed into silence.

Footfalls clomped off into the distance.

Nothing else registered but the pounding of her heart.

She grabbed the towel next to her, balled it around her fist, and struck the mirror. Shards of glass clinked into the ceramic sink, and on the green tiled floor. She picked up the largest shard. *If I'm going to survive, I'm going to need a weapon.* She told herself.

She held the shard of glass up—her gaze met her reflection; there was a determination in her eyes. The shard of mirror also caught something else; a dark shape moving in the foreground. She turned toward the window and her breath caught in her throat.

"Anna... are you still there?"

"Y-yes." she whimpered.

"Are you sure Frank is dead? Could he have just gotten injured?"

"What are you saying, Jen?"

"I'm saying maybe something else happened... you sound stressed. Are you sure he's dead?"

THEM

"Jen... I'm sitting next to his body now. Oh god, it's awful..."

"What?"

"His throat... it's been sliced open. The cut is so fucking deep... Of course my husband is dead! How could you question me at a time like this! I can't believe I have to explain this to you!" she yelled.

The temperature in the room plummeted to a low, bitter frost.

"T-that's impossible... what the fuck..."

"Jen? Jen, what the hell is going on?"

"Frank is walking to my house now."

"What?"

The man across the street was definitely Frank. She recognized his stumpy torso. It provided a stark contrast with his long arms and legs. His white shirt was drenched in blood. The red cloth stuck to his beer belly. His hideous, flaxen skin stretched over a bony, aged face.

With each breath Jeanette took, Frank drew even closer to her front door. Under his feet were dark puddles. He whispered something to himself. He turned his head toward her–his face was locked in that same ear-to-ear grin. His eyes were completely vacant. All she could do was stand motionless as he

THEM

approached her front door.

"Jen? Are you still there? I'm so scared."

"Y-yes. Where are you?"

"There's..." she trembled, "there's someone in the house. I've locked myself in the bedroom."

Jeanette exhaled a sigh of relief, "Good. Stay there. And do not, under any circumstances, open that door for anyone. Understood?"

"B-but..."

"Anna!"

"Y-yes... Jen, I'm s-so scared."

I know, me too, she thought. Except she couldn't say that. She couldn't afford to let Anna know that. She had to be strong for them both.

"Listen to me. We're going to get out of this. We will find a way to get through this night, okay? I promise you."

"Promise?"

"Yes. Just stay put, I need to think."

She looked down at her phone–the battery icon on the top right was red. She cursed herself for not having the wherewithal to charge it–but how could she have anticipated any of this?

"Anna, my phone is about to die. I'm going to try calling the police. Okay? Stay put. I've got you.

THEM

Promise."

"Alright... thank you."

Jeanette quickly hung up the call and dialed 9-1-1. The phone rang once, and then someone started speaking.

Jeanette's relief, however, was short lived.

"9-1-1. Sorry, we are unable to speak with you at this time due to the influx of calls we've been receiving. If this is an emergency, we advise you to stay on hold and an operator will be with you soon."

"Shit!"

She knew she didn't have time to wait. She killed the call and tried again, only to be met with the same result. It took everything in her to not fling the damn thing to the floor. The oppressive silence wormed its way into her anxious consciousness.

She got on all-fours and peeked under the door. Her eyes adjusted; she could make out the layout of the living room through the small crack. There were no signs of Brandon. The area was completely still.

Has he–or whatever that was–given up and gone to another house?

She tucked the shard of glass into her pocket, and slowly stood up. She opened the door a crack, letting her eyes adjust to the darkness.

THEM

Stillness.

Nothing moved an inch.

She anticipated her attacker... but found his absence to be even more unsettling. The house was completely empty. A boulder of dread sat on her shoulders. She kept the shard of glass tucked in her pocket and took a reluctant step past the door's threshold. The wooden floor groaned underneath the pressure of her steps. Dampness eased its way between her toes.

She guided the flashlight down.

Black liquid stained the floor.

It came from behind her.

She wheeled around and caught sight of the wet trail leading to the door of the basement. *Don't go down there*, she thought. She bent down and touched the fluid. Holding her hand up to the phone's light, her finger was tinted a shade of crimson.

Blood? What?

Her hands went numb. Pins and needles squirmed beneath the membrane of her flesh. She held her phone out to the open door of the basement, revealing the dark maw which led to the unending staircase. As she walked closer to it, a distinct crackling sound bellowed from deep below.

She pointed the light toward the entrance, but it

THEM

wasn't strong enough to illuminate what lurked deep in the shadows. All she could make out was the repulsive sound of waterlogged branches snapping. Just then, an unholy screech from the bowels of hell emanated from the inky depths.

Then came a thud, followed by another hideous shriek.

The crunching sound of frozen meat being put through a woodchipper grew louder as she began to finally see something touch the tip of her light.

It was the top of a blonde boy's head.

She squinted her eyes in an effort to clearly make out what it was. Until it jumped up at her. She fell backward, the air knocked clean from her chest. As she coughed in a breath, she focused the shaking beam of light in front of her as the blonde boy's head protruded from the basement's opening.

Except it wasn't a blonde boy.

The whiskers, the nose, the furry curls of chest hair...

The gaping laceration that ran from his chest to his crotch elicited a frantic wail from Jeanette. Tears welled up in her eyes at the sight of the ribbons of entrails dangling left and right from the belly she used to rub. The chestnut eyes that stared at her with all the love in the world had been viciously excavated from his

THEM

skull. His jaw—which she used to tickle—had been completely torn off. The tongue that licked her cheeks with more affection than she'd ever known drooped down with nothing to support it.

Brandon held Nico up by the neck.

The pet she loved like a son was dead, and the demon responsible for it grinned at her from ear-to-ear.

Fury that would make the devil himself wince ignited in her core. A banshee howl tore from her throat as she gripped the shard of glass and charged at Brandon with reckless abandon. She buried the jagged edge into his throat.

Nico fell to the floor in a gaudy splat. The grin etched into Brandon's face slowly receded as creamy gouts bubbled from his quivering lips. His eyes rolled to the back of his head as he fell backward, crashing down the stairs.

Jeanette collapsed to her knees, hunched over, and screamed into the abyss.

She wanted to cradle Nico in her arms, but she couldn't bring herself to even look at him. She wasn't the kind of person who could look into the caskets when she attended funerals because she only wanted to remember the good times she'd spent with the deceased. Now, she was confronted with not just the

THEM

death—but the vicious mauling that led up to it.

Taking in a sharp breath, she slapped the ground and hefted herself up. Her legs buckled under her, yet she managed to gather herself and stand steady. She slammed the basement door shut and hooked the latch.

Another loud series of raps pounded on the door. She darted toward the kitchen and unsheathed the largest knife she could find. She considered herself a bleeding-heart liberal and hated guns. She'd vowed to never own one.

She regretted that stance now.

When push came to shove, she needed something better than a knife to defend herself—something that would maintain a good distance between her and her attacker. She peered out the window and saw that the Frank imitator was trying to get in—he flashed that same nauseating, dead smile at her.

She mouthed "fuck you" at him and spat at the window.

She sprinted toward the backdoor and quietly shut it behind her. She scampered around the house, toward the front of the curb, and sprinted down the street. Her lungs and muscles burned under the agonizing work she suddenly demanded of them. She wasn't all that

THEM

physically active—she wasn't the type to work out and go to the gym because of how drained she was after a long work day. The only thing she did that vaguely qualified as exercise was walking Nico.

Nico.

Her chest compressed.

THEM
CHAPTER 3

Jeanette couldn't afford to stop running, so she kept at it. She barreled down the street, toward the next lane, made a right, and kept on as the flesh of her bare feet scraped the coarse cement. She had no idea of her destination; all she knew was that she had to get as far away from here as possible.

She stopped to catch her breath on the cold, wet pavement. Her feet were shredded and damp with blood and rainwater.

Out here, she was a sitting duck, and she needed a place to hide. She shot a quick glance around the street—her gaze caught a rectangular form in the distance. She hauled herself up and started toward it. It was a 'For Sale' sign. The house was likely vacant—and if this was an empty house, then there was no one in it to satiate the demons' bloodlust.

...Right?

Indifferently gazing down at Jeanette was a towering structure. An old, collapsed building that nature had taken over. Tendrils of vines trailed up the marble walls like green tree snakes. She tried the doorknob and, sure enough, it was unlocked. Stepping into the dilapidated structure's foyer, the subtle stench of creeping wood rot

THEM

wafted through the air.

She gently shut the door behind her, switched off the phone's flashlight, and swiped up to the call screen. She typed in 9-1-1 and held it to her ear.

It didn't ring.

"What the fuck..." she whispered to herself as a shiver ran through her body.

The silence was just as disconcerting as the laughs.

She crouched, got on her knees, and kneeled in front of the window. Three humanoid figures lurched far in the distance of the foggy street. One limped as the others maintained that same pace next to it. Part of her wanted to approach them on the off chance they were survivors. Her better judgment, however, begged her to trust *no one*.

She checked her phone—the battery was now at 5%.

In the darkness, she felt eyes crawling up her body. Was this her sixth sense warning her of another being's presence, or was this just helpless paranoia? The ability to distinguish one from the other alluded her.

A pulsating, electric current ran under the floorboards.

She slipped her phone back into her pocket and groped around for purchase. Her hand landed on a cold surface that she used to haul herself back to her feet.

THEM

She maintained the straight path she was on, hoping to find a doorknob to a room she could stay in for the night. At the very least, she wondered if there was a staircase she could climb just to put more space between her and *them*.

"Hey."

"Fuck!" Jeanette nearly jumped out of her skin.

"Shhh. Please, keep it down."

Jeanette ran toward the door, but a hand clamped over her mouth. She bucked and thrashed, but the person's grip was unrelenting.

"Please stop, I'm not one of them," a woman hissed.

A chill ran over her body at the prospect of how well these things could imitate voices.

Can I trust her? Am I actually willing to place my trust in a stranger? Someone who wore the face of a man I know just tried to kill me...

"I'm gonna let you go, okay? Please don't scream. I'm unarmed."

Jeanette weighed the options in her head. She had the advantage because she was holding a knife while both the stranger's hands tried to restrain her. Even if this stranger wielded a weapon, she'd still have to access it.

Jeanette nodded.

Instantly, the woman loosened up her grip. Jeanette

THEM

spun around, facing the stranger's general direction. She could barely make her features out, but the faint outline she could detect revealed that her hands were in the air in surrender.

"Please. I'm scared. I live a couple of blocks away... it was actual chaos."

"How do I know I can trust you?"

"I could ask the same of you, ya know?"

Touché.

"Well... I don't know what to tell you. Look, I'm just going to find another place to lay low, alright? If you're one of *them*, I don't want to be around you. And if you aren't, well..."

"Well?"

"I don't like my chances, alright? I'm just going to go..."

Jeanette started toward the door, but the woman grabbed her by the arm.

"Bitch, I have a knife!" Jeanette shrieked.

"Sorry, sorry..." the woman sounded terrified, "I just don't want to be alone, okay?"

Despite the darkness, Jeanette could tell the woman was crying. The sniffling sounds, and the way her hand trembled as it was still wrapped around her wrist... Jeanette turned on the phone's flashlight and pointed it

THEM

at the woman. Her face twisted in confusion and fear. There was life in her eyes; genuine emotion that fell on Jeanette like a thin blanket of reassurance.

The woman also had a protruding belly.

She was pregnant.

"What are you–?... Turn that thing off."

"Sorry, I just had to see your eyes."

"What?"

"The guy who attacked me, he..." Jeanette sighed thinking about Nico, "his eyes were completely dead. There was something just so wrong about him. He wasn't human."

"I know. I was attacked too. I managed to escape but... just hours ago the entire fucking street was on fire. It was awful," she sniffs snot back.

"Did anyone you know get hurt?"

"Yeah... my brother Paul, he... I don't know what happened. I woke up to this loud banging sound. It was coming downstairs in the kitchen and, fuck..."

Jeanette stepped forward and wrapped the girl in a hug. The girl buried her head in Jeanette's shoulder and wept. It took everything in her to stifle back her own tears. After a few minutes, the cries subsided.

"... you see my dad was on a business trip, and he wasn't expected back until the end of next week. So

THEM

when I saw him... straddling my brother, stabbing him... I just..."

"Did you see his face?"

"Yeah, I did. He was smiling, but there was nothing in his eyes—it was the empty look he'd have when he did something like take out the trash... but his mouth was smiling."

"That wasn't your father."

"B-but I saw him..."

"I know what you saw, and I believe you. But I need you to believe me. The same thing just happened to me. This man who I thought I knew killed my dog. My neighbor's husband was also murdered... but he was walking around outside my house."

"What?"

"I don't know what's going on. Someone is impersonating people we love and trying to get to us. Trying to kill us..."

"Why?"

"I don't know."

"What the fuck is going on?" Her exasperation grew louder.

"Shh! We don't want any of them to hear us."

"Sorry, I..."

"What's your name?"

THEM

"Samantha."

"How many months in are you?"

"Just coming on seven..."

"Good. Alright, Samantha. Beautiful name. May I call you Sam?"

"S-sure... that's what my friends call me."

"Alright Sam, I'm Jeanette. And if your baby and you are going to survive this, we're going to have to try and keep a clear head, alright?"

"Yeah..."

"I'm sorry to hear about your brother. Were you guys close?"

"N-Not really. He's a lot younger, so we don't really have all that much in common. I had to move in with my folks because I need their help with this baby."

"I take it this child's father isn't..."

"Nah, he was a loser anyway. My daddy was right about him."

"Are you and your dad close?"

"Yeah, you could say that. I'm pretty close with both my parents, actually. We don't have much, but they've never complained. They were strict, but I guess I see where they're coming from now."

Jeanette hated small talk but engaging it in was all she could do to keep herself sane. She needed to hear

THEM

someone else speaking to distract herself because she couldn't bear to entertain her own thoughts any longer.

Nico... Brandon...

"I know what you mean, Sam. What do your parents do if you don't mind my asking?"

"Nah, no worries. Dad owns a hardware store, and mom is a waitress. He wanted her to be a stay-at-home kinda mom, but she had to work for our sake. And now with this baby, I feel even more like a burden."

"Listen, Sam. Your parents love you, alright? They love you more than you'll ever know."

"You think so?"

"Think about how much you love your baby. That's a parent's love for you."

"Thanks, Jeanette. I really appreciate that. You probably can't see me all that well, but I'm actually smiling."

Jeanette pulled her into another hug and gently patted her back.

"I think I'm going to explore upstairs. Give me your hand."

Samantha coyly took Jeanette's hand. She held the flashlight up to the room. It was an empty space bereft of furniture. Whoever owned this property clearly didn't live in it. It was uninhabitable. The windows

THEM

were flaked with dirt, the wooden beams overhead were strewn with cobwebs, and the cracked walls had moss growing on them. Her phone wasn't strong enough to light up the whole room, so she could only view it in fragments. They climbed the stairs leading to a hallway with a series of wooden doors.

"Creepy, huh?" Jeanette said.

"Yeah..."

"Hey, what time is it?"

"It's 3:10am... Saturday already."

"Damn."

She inspected the windows and saw that the back of this house overlooked the huge swath of uncut grass leading to the nearby woods. Jeanette must've ran further than she thought if she was already in this part of town. Through the corner of her eyes, she thought she caught glimpses of stealthy movements in the shadows of the trees.

It's nothing. There's nothing else out there, she told herself.

The stench of decay on this floor was thicker. The air seethed with the noxious odor of mildew and rot–the entire place had the pungent stench of a dead rat carcass. A faint hissing sound echoed across the room. It was in a state of utter disrepair. This floor had been

THEM

neglected to a startling degree—as if it had been left alone for an entire century.

Jeanette felt uneasy—a dreadful unease tugged at every hair follicle in her body.

The place looked like a den that had been ransacked by hookers and junkies. Jeanette drew the flashlight around: graffiti covered the walls, and the floor was littered with human feces and used needles. There were cobwebs on every corner, and the patches of floor that weren't littered with human waste were caked with dust. Its ceiling tiles had deteriorated into blackened husks from leaking rainwater.

Something scurried around in the corner.

It wouldn't surprise me if a place like this had a rat infestation.

Across them were a filthy pair of windows that beamed at her like the eyes of a hungry lion. Jeanette continued her exploration through a door across the second story landing. It led into a long, narrow hallway that extended to the front of the building. She checked behind the ajar doors; behind one was a musty bathroom, behind another was a dusty kitchenette. These rooms, like the rest of the house, had been left to rot in abandoned squalor.

Footsteps creaked in the distance.

THEM

They were light, deliberate footfalls punctuated by the worn groans and squeaks of old wooden flooring. Her flashlight could only illuminate so much. Maybe it was her mind playing tricks on her, but the darkness up ahead seemed to grow thicker in her vision.

A shiver ran down Jeanette's spine. She shook her head like she was trying to loosen a thought trapped inside.

She turned around to check on Samantha.

Samantha wasn't there.

"Samantha..." Jeanette said under her breath.

No response.

Jeanette stormed toward the hall, terrified that something could have harmed Samantha. She sauntered past the bathroom, past the kitchenette, hastily glancing into each room to make sure Samantha hadn't been hiding in it either. She cursed herself for letting this young woman out of her sight. As much as she detested it, she couldn't help but feel lost without her.

Turning her head, she quickly was met with the sight of an empty room. She unlocked her phone and checked the time. 4:17am. There was something so unsettling about being in a house when it was empty–even back at her place, she had had Nico to keep her

THEM

company.

Where the fuck is she?

Every one of Jeanette's footsteps was amplified by the silence. Even the exhalation of her breath seemed deafening in the wide space.

"Hello?" she called out, desperate to get some sort of response.

Nothing came.

Jeanette ran back into the hallway, double-checking the kitchenette and bathroom.

Samantha was in neither.

Violently spinning around and trying to make sense of it all, tears welled in her eyes. *You have to keep it together*, she told herself. She slapped herself in the face, only to howl in pain when the full weight of the blow connected with her cheek. She cupped her hand to her cheek which stung from the ruthless strike.

Rubbing her forehead, she tried to think of something else. Her best bet, she thought, was to just lock herself in one of the rooms and wait this out until morning.

But what if they've already gotten to Samantha and already know you're here? What if Samantha was one of them and she'd been deceiving me all this time?

Ambling down the stairs, Jeanette found no one. She could've sworn she heard footsteps not too long ago,

THEM

but there seemed to be no source it could have originated from. Jeanette involuntarily balled her hands into fists. There was no tangible threat in her immediate sight, yet her stomach churned like she was being stalked by a bloodthirsty killer.

"Samantha?"

All she received was the sound of silence.

Her skin crawled, goosebumps formed. It was almost as if she wished one of *them* were in there with her—at least that would validate her concerns and push her to some kind of action. A small part of her suspected she was dreaming, but she knew she wasn't. She'd just slapped herself in the face, she was awake, and this night terror was real.

She did the only thing she could and walked back up the stairs.

She couldn't hear anything giving chase behind her, yet the thick concentration of dread refused to dilute. She walked past the door, past the kitchenette and the bathroom, all the way down the hall to the furthest side of the building. She could've sworn that, in her haste, she'd stepped on a used syringe.

Everything in front of her was still.

There was an energy, and overwhelming force of some sort that gave her the urge to cut her losses and just run

THEM

out of the house. She fought against it as much as she could. Yet, she couldn't bear to be alone any longer. She didn't want to go back into those streets where *they* lurked, but she also didn't want to find out what else hid in the innards of this filthy structure with her.

Jeanette recalled another tip her father told her to help manage her anxiety.

Look around the room and name the objects you see.

She held up the phone flashlight and assessed her surroundings. The wooden floor was partially eaten by termites; the plaster of the ceiling had holes which exposed the veins of water pipes lining the building's inner workings; there was hardly any swath of wall that wasn't infested by cobwebs. The sounds of rodents scurrying added to the overall dreariness.

Every second was an eternity in this filthy, isolated space. She needed to hear the sound of something else, anything else. Anything but that damned silence would've helped.

Jeanette slumped to her knees, defeated.

"Boo!"

The sheer auditory thrust of that voice made Jeanette's heart leap out of her chest.

"Fuck damn it!"

Jeanette's body surged with anger at this petulant

THEM

child's games. It took everything in her to muster up the patience to force herself to reel it back in. She couldn't afford to lose an ally. She told herself that Samantha was just a kid, and that perhaps humor was her way of coping with this whole situation.

"Woah, sorry! I didn't mean to spook you... I just wanted to lighten the mood."

"Oh, fuck off."

"Hey, I said I was sorry. Jeez, lighten up."

"My dog was killed in front of me."

"Fuck..."

"Yeah, I just played the dead dog card."

"I understand if you want to leave me, I–"

"I'm fucking with you Sam," she said, in a half-hearted effort to lighten the mood, "but for real–no jump-scares from now on."

Samantha let out a soft chuckle, clearly under the impression that Jeanette had cracked a joke. She hadn't. Jeanette needed to make it clear, right now, that there were to be no more games for the rest of the evening. She fucking hated surprises. She wanted to keep the mood light, but she also needed to be stern enough to be understood. She snapped around, pointing the flashlight at Samantha, only for her entire body to freeze in fear.

THEM

The light cast on the wall in front of her had three shadows.

The wall behind Samantha should've only had one.

Jeanette's face froze in a mask of terror. Behind Samantha was a man. She didn't recognize his face, but she certainly recognized that petrifying grin. The man stood as still as a mannequin. A million thoughts zipped through her mind at light speed.

Was he here this whole time? How did he move without being heard?

She wanted to scream, to warn Samantha, but her words were lodged in her fear-parched throat.

"What?" Samantha said.

Before Jeanette could say anything, the man slapped his hand over Samantha's mouth and yanked her toward him. She thrashed, bucked forward and back, but was unable to escape his oppressive grip. Jeanette clenched the handle of the knife and lunged forward. Just then, footsteps thudded behind her and another man ensnared Jeanette in his muscular pair of arms.

"Fuck you! Fuck you! Let me go, you fucking bastard." Jeanette screamed.

A slippery slug-like texture brushed along Jeanette's cheek. A tongue. This man's breath smelled like days-old meat that had been left out. She tried to gain

THEM

purchase, but he thrashed her around. The light of the flashlight frantically darted around the room like a strobe. He locked her in a sort of sleeper hold.

"You move one inch, bitch, and I'll snap your neck."

"Yeah? What kind of fun would it be to you if I was dead?"

He gripped her neck so tight, her chest burned with the lack of oxygen she was getting. Her skull throbbed in agony, and her eyes swelled to the point of being moments away from popping out of their sockets. He loosened the grip slightly, just so she could cough in a shallow series of breaths.

"I'm gonna keep you alive, you cocksucking slut. For now. I just need you to watch what's about to happen. If I catch you looking away, I'll pop your pretty pink clit with this,"

He held a rusted pair of scissors up to her face.

"Just try it, you fucking bitch. I'll fuck you with these here scissors–I'll shove this knife so far up your cunt you'll feel it behind your nice titties."

Tears welled up in Jeanette's eyes. It couldn't be helped–all she could do was nod, and so she did. In front of her, Samantha was wailing uncontrollably.

"Jamie, stop!" Samantha said.

"Wait, what?"

THEM

"Jeanette... that's my brother. He must've followed me."

"She's moving around too much!" the man restraining Samantha barked.

"Daddy?" Samantha said, weeping.

"Oh yes, daddy's here."

"And mommy is here, too." A woman with a crackly voice said.

"Mommy, daddy? Why? I thought you loved me. What did I do wrong? Please, I beg you... I'll get the abortion like you said!"

"It's too late for that now, you dumb slut!"

"I'll put it up for adoption! Just please let me go!"

"Shut the fuck up, cunt."

"I bet this bitch would make a real good punching bag."

A pulpy *thwack* bounced off the walls. It sounded again and again. Samantha was being pummeled within an inch of her life.

"No, not my baby! Please!"

"Turn her into a head on a stick."

The woman passing as Samantha's mother buried a knife into the top of Samantha's back, straight into the top of her spinal cord. With that, Samantha's helpless body slackened. There was no movement save for the

THEM

expression on her face that shifted from horror to hopelessness.

"Please!" She yelped, "I don't wanna die... I don't wanna die!"

Jeanette wanted to close her eyes. She knew that doing so would spell the death of her. She stayed as still as possible and used her fingers to ease the knife out of her belt strap as she watched, in abject terror.

Unholy shrieks bellowed out of Samantha as she repeated that same line to the point of incoherence. Her babbling turned into screams as the woman's serrated knife gouged into her flesh, digging deeper until a stream of blood drained out of the fresh gash. The knife was wielded with no skill–it inelegantly sawed into Samantha's skin, separating membrane from bone and muscle. She cut down to her cheek, exposing the network of tissue and muscle beneath.

Samantha's screams turned hoarse. The blade worked through the skin beneath her left eye, scraping against the bone of her nose, and up across her forehead, then down the opposite side of her face. The sawing motion went back and forth. The top half of Samantha's face folded over her mouth. Her eyes stared at Jeanette with nothing to blink with. When the rubbery flap of skin reached her neck, her eyes rolled to the back of her

THEM

head. The smiling man who posed as her father gripped her skin and yanked it off her face like it was a mask. It tore away in one piece. He dangled the face above the woman's mouth, letting blood drip on her tongue.

"Get her pants off!"

"On it."

The fiend unbuttoned her shorts and yanked them down. He then took a broken shard of glass from the floor and parted her limp legs.

"What? What are you doing?" Samantha sobbed.

"On second thought, I think I am going to let my trashy, back-talking daughter have an abortion. And it ain't gonna cost me a single cent!"

Jeanette gasped, feeling the second-hand pain as the man plunged the glass into Samantha's vaginal canal.

He laughed like a maniac, pulling the jagged shard of glass out just so he could ram it in deeper. He thrusted and twisted it into her rhythmically, devastating the elastic musculature. Jeanette's breath caught in her throat at the notion that he could possibly stab the innocent baby's head.

Samantha's screams were hoarse and unending. If she had any control of her body, she'd no doubt be trying to squeeze her legs together. Instead, she had to just lie there as her womanhood was eviscerated beyond

THEM

recognition. Her labia looked like pulpy meat that had been mauled by a rabid dog.

"Alright, now for the fun part," he said, pointing at Jeanette's sweat-slicked face."

"And you better not look away, bitch."

All Jeanette could do was glare at *them*.

The man clenched his hand into a fist, grabbed Samantha by the hair and jabbed blow after blow right at her pregnant belly. Samantha shrieked and then let out a labored series of heavy coughs. The woman laughed maniacally, tugging at Samantha's blood-stained hair.

The man then tossed the glass aside and forced his hand past Samantha's destroyed entrance. He jerked his wrist upward and in, ignoring the broken glass that bit into his skin. His arm dug into her, well past his wrist, until he eventually hit something. He yanked his hand out, producing gastric, farting noises. It slid out like an oil-slicked glove, taking clumps of tissue and muscle with it. Viscous sludge spurted out her beefy cunt like bubbling cherry syrup. He shoved his hand back in and ripped out a leg that looked like it was nothing more than a clump of red slime.

He unfurled the specimen, revealing the shape of a malformed fetus.

THEM

"Time to show my grandson how babies are made!"

He pried open the abortion's legs and plunged his erect prick into the baby's anus. He gripped the infant's legs as he pumped in and out of its blue, lifeless body. The fetus' mouth opened as the man's enormous cock pierced through its body and poked out of its throat.

"I think I've worked me up an appetite!" The woman said.

She pulled the baby off the man's cock and bit into its face, tearing a chunk clean off. The man stroked his cock at Samantha's skinned face. A jet of musky liquid streamed out of his cock, landing all over Samantha's face. She choked and made gargling sounds as the ribbons of cum landed in her mouth. The stream of ejaculation concluded in intermittent, conclusive spurts landing on her eyes. Her head looked like glazed, meaty soup. All she could muster up were a series of helpless moans.

The woman then dug her thumb into the baby's eye socket and squeezed. Blood bubbled out from beneath the grip of her sharp nails.

A strong cramp seized Jeanette's stomach. She held her breath in an effort to hold back the rising upchuck.

Blood sprayed out of the fetus's mouth in thick hazes. She then crushed the infant's sternum, causing more

THEM

gooey meat to belch out of its gaping, violated asshole. Out came threads of gooey blood and purple entrails. She held the baby over her head, bit into the intestines, and ravenously slurped them into her starving maw. Organs spewed out of the infant's rectum like an oyster being sucked from its shell. She then stuck her fingers into the baby's rectum, digging into where its mutilated innards once were.

"Time to make some baby paste!"

With one quick motion, she tore the infant in half, without a hint of effort. Its milky skin skimmed and slid through bones, biting sharply into the resistant cartilage and sinew. Hot blood spurted out of each half and dribbled on the floor.

It had utterly ceased to be human. All it was now two split ends of meaty leftovers and fleshy tendons that secreted puddles of blood. The smell violated Jeanette's olfactory senses with the acerbic bite of fungal growth from an expired rat carcass.

The man then bent over Samantha's uncovered eye and planted his mouth over it. He sucked in with savage slurps–the noise was akin to a burp being stifled by sealed lips. His cheeks hollowed as he sucked her orbital juices in. He took the sound of a *pop* as his cue to jerk his head back.

THEM

A strand of red muscle connected his puckered lips to her empty socket. Chunks of thick blood fell from the excavated hole in her head and spattered onto her breasts.

"Stick it in! Stick it in that fuckin' ugly cow!" The man who posed as Jamie howled.

The fiend's member had instantly stiffened again. He grabbed Samantha by the skull and impaled her hemorrhaging eye socket with his stiff prick. Her mewling turned to gags as gouts of blood coughed up from her throat. He pumped in and out of her head, thrusting with the force of a jackhammer. Bits of gray brain matter oozed out of her nose with squelching sounds of grapes being trampled on.

"Oh shit I'm gonna fuckin' nut again!"

"Hell yeah, bust that fuckin' load in that slut's skull!"

His body halted to a series of shakes as he climaxed into Samantha's brutalized head cavity. Samantha puked out creamy brain matter and gore. She keeled over as nuggets of red bile and torn tissue fell out of her slackened jaw.

By then, Jeanette's adrenaline had been heightened beyond madness, and her heart pounded in her chest like a hammer striking hot iron. The knife was now fully loosened from her belt, she gripped it in her hand

THEM

and swung it behind her. The blade made contact—a geyser of blood sprayed over her.

She tore the blade free. Sprung upward and ran past the glass window, shattering it. She landed on the arch right under her, then rolled off it to the sodden grass on the lawn. The wind was knocked out of her, and for a second she thought she'd shattered her spine and got paralyzed. She took a sharp breath and moved her foot.

She was alright.

Stunned, but alive.

She caught sight of the erratic shadows slinking in the dim light of the window she'd just burst out of.

"Fuck!" She yelled, as she realized that light came from her phone which must've fallen as she struggled. She now had no way of communicating. She was all alone once again; it was just her and her knife.

In the window, the man's bloody face stared down at her, it was illuminated from the light below him, and the effect was bone-chilling.

He had a lump of meat in his mouth, and his entire torso was stained with dark liquid. Jeanette squinted to make out what it was. It was a heart. Samantha's once beating heart. The ghoul bit deeper into the dead muscle as thick juices squirted out of it.

THEM

The rain had since stopped, and the clouds overhead spread thin. The crescent-shaped moon was now vaguely visible and casting a dim light over the town. In the distance were a series of shrill howls coming from every angle. She didn't feel safe out here. *They* were attracted to people. *The houses had people, the woods didn't,* she thought.

Jeanette pivoted, sprinted to the back of the house, and dashed into the woods.

THEM
CHAPTER 4

Her trek into the brushy gloom of the forest wasn't something she'd planned or anticipated. At this point she was so far in; she couldn't tell which way was North and which was South. For all she knew, she was walking around in circles.

Above her was a thick canopy of gnarled trees misshapen by the monsoon. She'd long since scampered away from the beaten path and was now dodging branches and groping for patches of ground that weren't littered with jagged stones.

She stopped at the foot of a hill and looked back. The path behind her gaped like the dark maw of a withered crone post rigor mortis. The whole atmosphere was depressing and sullen. Crickets chirped in the trees as a flock of bats unleashed a chorus of piercing cries.

Were they bats or ...

"Jeanette."

The deep, gravelly sound of a man billowed through the wind, bouncing off the trees.

"Jeanette..."

She ran further into the woods, forcing herself to trust that this was all in her head–that this was all just her mind playing cruel tricks on her in a desperate attempt

THEM

at self-preservation.

Yet her name still echoed down from the bramble of branches above, raining down on her like an acid drizzle.

"Jeanette..."

"Jeanette..."

Please, please, please let it just be my imagination.

She tried to reason with herself–but what was the reason in a world as unreasonable as this? Perhaps she was the insane one.

The volume of trees grew thicker. Each tree looked like the one she'd just seen an hour ago. Has it already been an hour? Her arms brushed against the fungus-strewn bark, as fallen branches and twigs stabbed her bare feet.

"Jeanette... Jeanette... Jeanette..."

There was that blasted voice again. This time it was louder; this time it overlapped with another voice. There were several people in the woods with her.

"It's all in your head. It's all in your head. It's all in your head..." she whispered to herself, wrapping her arms around her body to placate the onslaught of chills.

Confused and frightened, she snuggled up in an alcove between the hollow portion of a rotting tree's

THEM

bark. Her heart slammed into the back of her chest. She considered her breathing exercises, but she didn't want to risk being heard. She instead clamped her hand over her mouth and took shallow breaths. She thanked her lucky stars that the moon was behind her, thus, the alcove was shrouded in darkness. The dim night served as a cloak, yet the only thing that really shielded her from *them* were the cobwebs strewn across the wood in front of her.

Her chest tightened at the sudden accumulation of bizarre scratching noises coming from every which way. Eventually, she noticed the clear outline of her hand. She gazed up–the sky began to gray, signaling the incoming dawn.

She hadn't gotten a wink of sleep.

Her hiding spot was useless now. The noises had since subsided, and she couldn't risk cornering herself in this same spot, so she slowly eased her way out.

Did I fall asleep?

Her mouth was parched, and her vision was foggy. If she had slept, the details of her dreams would have already eluded her. They'd faded away like the last droplets of dew on the leaves her legs brushed against. *Has my dream been one of a better world?* She thought. Hard as she tried, she couldn't place it.

THEM

When she was in college, she had pulled all-nighters almost every week. Yet now, at her age—with the job she worked—she was exhausted all the time. Even if she had gotten some sleep, her face still prickled with exhaustion.

She took a step forward, but a branch clicked under her foot. The noise was so loud it echoed across the unsaturated gloom.

Something darted into the bushes.

In the midst of an unseasonably cold night, she could vaguely make out her breath clouding in front of her.

She took this as her signal to dive into the path before her, casting aside the onslaught of bushes and trees. She ran for what felt like another few hours, casting sideway glances to see if there were any signs of life.

Her throat tightened past the point of comfort. The path in front of her was dense, yet she willed herself with every last spark of energy to forge ahead and plunged into the sunless greenery. Forward, her heartbeat reverberated through her bones, her sights set exclusively on the dull glimmers of light. The noises around her faded, the branches a haze. She told herself that freedom was within reach—she just had to keep pushing.

A cover of fatigue folded over her—she slapped herself

THEM

in the face to wake herself up. She knew that this was a matter of life and death. Any form of complicity would result in her undoing.

She scrambled and climbed ahead. A sharp jolt of pain jounced up the back of her leg. She paused and hinged forward to examine the source—a thick spine of wood had embedded itself into her bare heel. Panic stricken and paralyzed with fear, she lifted up her heel, pinched the earthly needle, and wrenched it out. Blood pulsed out of her foot, sending shockwaves to all four corners of its sole. She wanted to stop and nurse her wound, but she couldn't; doing so would place her in considerably more harm.

The lighter the sky, the thinner the leafy murk in front of her became.

A clearing appeared a short distance ahead. She had arrived at the point of the woods where the earth met the road. Just then, another thrum of feet reverberated in the prison of trees; it was followed by a low, grumbling murmur...

"Jeanette..."

"JeanetteJeanetteJeanetteJeanetteJeanette..."

The gravelly voices came from everywhere. Her heart raced as she snapped her head back, frantically trying to locate the source of these sounds.

THEM

The woods were still.

She chided herself for this action, for it was an inadvertent concession that this was *actually* happening. It wasn't all in her head. Somewhere, out there, a relentless pursuer was on her trail.

She headed toward the road and stopped in the middle of the damp, ice-cold gravel.

Up ahead was what looked like an abandoned grain factory. On the eastern side of the woods was a road that cut between a series of houses and a gas station. Beyond that was fog so thick she couldn't see past it.

The houses on the other side of the block appeared to be unkempt and abandoned. They looked as if they hadn't been occupied even prior to the events of last night.

A thick layer of dust covered their cracked windows; it was impossible to see inside. One house had a porch completely littered with cobwebs and mold. The lawn had grass that reached knee-level.

Even from where she stood, the aroma of melted sap and mothballs invaded her senses. This looked like a movie set—a street built to create the most debased horror tales.

When she finally managed to unhook her gaze from the houses, her heart stopped.

THEM

The sudden shock felt like her body had just jumped twenty feet off the puddled concrete. Some of the fog had been pushed back by the wind, and far in the distance stood about twenty people. They were frozen like posed mannequins.

What unnerved her was the notion that they could've easily let their presence be known. Instead, they simply glared at her as they maintained their distance. Their blank expressions sent more shivers of dread down her spine.

A cold sweat congealed on her chest as her stomach churned with unease.

At first glance, they appeared to be normal people. The vast stretch of suburban houses behind them made the entire scene look like a Norman Rockwell painting that had been filtered through a negative filter. *They* were a mix of men, women, and children–though not a single one of them seemed alive. Their faces were familiar–she'd seen those children playing hopscotch on the streets; she'd seen those women at the grocery store; she'd seen several of those men coming out of their cars and greeting their wives after a long day's work.

Jeanette trudged backward, keeping her gaze firmly latched onto them. She held her breath, trying to pacify

THEM

her surging lungs. She swallowed a gulp so large it was as if she'd forced down an entire plum. She felt like an unwelcome visitor, ambling with bated breath as this army of strangers stared at her in silence. She felt like a rat in a laboratory–*they* were the mad scientists who coldly studied her every movement.

She caught the eye of one man making direct eye contact with her.

Run. Now.

But she couldn't.

She knew how fast these beings were; she knew how stealthily they'd snuck up on her and Samantha just the night before.

A smile cracked on the man's face.

All the hair in her body stood–her teeth chattered. A dull ache throbbed between her eyes as blood rushed to her head with immense pressure.

You have to go. You have to go.

Her fingers tightened so much around the hilt of the knife that her knuckles went white.

Her sweat-slicked hand shook in terror.

The smiling man's head cracked to the side–his mouth stood at odds with his eyes which glowered at her with barbarous intent. His gaze was glacial and piercing; it stabbed so deep into her core that she felt

THEM

like he was looking right through her.

The man began to convulse as his joints cracked. He belted out a screech so thundering, she had to cover her ears. The shriek then contorted into a laugh from hell. It bounced off the houses and echoed throughout the entire street. The pitch was akin to the mating call of a banshee.

Then he advanced, sprinting toward her.

Alarm set in as she spun around and sprinted toward the factory. The soles of her feet dug into the wet cement—her labored breathing surged as she tore down the street. She didn't dare look back; the sound of an entire stampede was closing in on her.

The laughs proliferated like an artificial voice generator had short circuited and played on an endless loop.

The dilapidated structures zipped by her as she sprinted. They towered around her like hulking, ancient sentinels raring out of the darkness. She sucked in as much air as she could and kept running, breaking stride as she dodged the potholes. She kicked her way through the debris-littered street as she continued forward, the heavy tread of *their* footsteps echoed behind her.

Another series of howling guffaws were let loose in

THEM

what felt like a calculated effort to scare her.

It worked.

She screamed, glancing back to see that they'd now gotten closer. She averted her gaze back to the factory– back to her end goal. Even the slightest instance of stalling would prove to be fatal. The factory grew larger with every stride.

Her heartbeat thundered in her ears.

Her lungs burned; her chest felt like a sack of bricks had just been dropped on it. She desperately sucked in as much air as she could, but it was never enough. Her feet seared under the pressure, and her eyes felt like they were about to implode into the back of her aching skull. Her thoughts raced to her father, to Janice... she stood inches away from the factory door. Crying out again, she reached the door and hurled herself forward with everything she had left.

The massive, rusting door, wedged open upon impact. The second she slid into the crack, she snapped around and bolted the latch shut. An infantry of fists pounded on the metal, causing the entire structure to quiver.

She took a few steps back and sucked in the deepest breath she'd ever taken as she fell to the floor.

The chase had ended, but her quest for survival was nowhere near over. The latch was a hulking metal rod

THEM

that ran from one end of the door to the other. There was no way they would be able to break though... or so she hoped.

"Fuck... you..." she rasped.

Dawn had broken now. Glistening light peered through the decrepit windows.

THEM
CHAPTER 5

The factory was rusting and old, but it still seemed to keep the same structure of when it had been built.

She explored the ground floor.

It was enormous–probably the largest single room she'd ever been in. Above her were so many levels, bridges, and catwalks. The antechamber was filled with rusted, unkempt turbines and generators covered in dust and rubble. All the buttons and levers were worn with age.

She took another step forward and felt the sudden coolness of metal press against her throat.

"Don't make any more sudden movements, bitch."

"I'm–" she gulped.

"Shut the fuck up" The woman said, "get on your fucking knees and put your hands up."

Jeanette was relieved that the request was clearly something that had come from a lucid human being– she couldn't blame them for their rage and distrustfulness. She complied. She got on one knee, and then the other. She raised her arms, feeling the cramping compression in her back from being in that wooden alcove.

"Look at me," the woman barked.

THEM

Jeanette looked up. Her eyes came into contact with the rays of the sun. She almost dropped her hand to shield them but didn't want to risk incurring this woman's ire. Jeanette shut her eyes after getting a good look at her.

She's a tall, fit woman who looked to be in her late twenties. Her long, wavy blonde hair was draped over her shoulder. She wore a tank top and slim-fit sweatpants. In one hand was a hunting knife–in the other, a gun.

The barrel of the gun was aimed at Jeanette's face.

"Who are you and what are you doing here?"

"My name is Jeanette. I didn't intend on coming here but I was chased into the woods and down the street, I didn't have anywhere to go, I–"

"Woah, slow down."

Jeanette realized that she was speaking a million words a minute–her voice mirrored the frenetic pace of her anxious mind. She paused, took a deep breath, and continued.

"Sorry... My name is Jeanette, I was–"

"Yeah, yeah, Jeanette. I got that. What happened to you and how did you find this place?"

She paused to recall the events of the previous evening–cataloged and compartmentalized them in her

THEM

head, trimming away the unnecessary fat. She needed to be as succinct and intelligible as possible.

Slow down, she told herself.

"Last night, during the storm, an emergency broadcast system showed on TV," the mention of this caused a spark in the woman's eye, "then the power went out, and all this shit started happening..."

"Yeah, we got that too."

"We?"

"Hold up, I'm not done with you yet. Keep going."

"Okay so this man I know showed up to my house. I-I was under the impression that he wasn't even in the state... so for him to show up unannounced–something he'd never done before–I knew something was wrong. And then my dog, my..."

Tears welled up in Jeanette's eyes. She forced herself to forget the image of Nico's disemboweled body. Though the more she tried to stifle it, the more that vile image forced itself into her head. She attempted to fight back the tears, but her efforts were for naught. She bawled out all the emotion she'd built up. She heaved breathy sobs as snot dripped down to her upper lip. It took everything in her to not bring her hands to her hideously misshapen face.

"I think I can make out the rest..." The woman's voice

THEM

trailed off.

Jeanette attempted to respond, but the sobs stifled her words. She wished Nico was here to comfort her. He was her lovable companion who could sense when she was sad–whenever she'd been having a bad day, he knew to curl up next to her and rest his soft head on her lap. All she had left of him was the repugnant image of his entrails sweeping the floor.

"I'll n-never see him a-again... I'll..."

"Alright, stand up and spread your arms apart."

Jeanette nodded, then slowly complied. The woman searched her body, stopping at her side. She pulled the knife away, then sheathed it into her belt.

"I'm not one of them, you have to believe me. Please..."

"I believe you. I just need to be sure, so I'm going to have to take this. Is that going to be a problem?"

Is she serious? Does she know what being unarmed in a world like this could mean? Still, Jeanette couldn't afford to be testy.

"N-no, it won't be a problem."

"Okay. Good. You can come with me. I'll walk behind you and guide you through."

Jeanette nodded and walked ahead, following the woman's instructions.

THEM

"I'm Shannon, by the way. We're going to meet up with my boyfriend, Alex. He's upstairs keeping a lookout."

"Nice to meet you, Shannon."

"Likewise. You can never tell who's a stiff and who isn't."

"Is that what they're called?"

"Don't know. That's just the name we gave them."

They ascended the staircase, and the quality of light began to improve. Atop the stairs was a large broken window. Encased in the rectangular frame was the silhouette of a man facing them.

"That's Alex."

Alex had pale skin, black hair, and deep-set gray eyes. Looking at both of them in the light, they both had dark circles under their eyes. Jeanette wasn't the only one who'd failed to get adequate rest. The exhaustion brought forth from her restless night made her want to lie down on the floor and close her eyes.

If I could just close my eyes for five minutes...

"Shan, are you crazy? What the fuck is this?"

"Relax. She's one of us."

"How do you know?"

"All you need to do is look in their eyes. The stiffs don't cry, and they definitely don't get on their knees

THEM

and hand over their weapons," she said, brandishing Jeanette's knife.

"I just need to... sit down." Jeanette's feeble voice barely escaped her.

"Yeah, go ahead. Sit over there where we can see you."

And so she did.

She rested her back against the wall behind her as she slid to the ground. The second she landed; she closed her eyes... Yet sleep eluded her. Her eyes were shut, her entire body was weighed down by debilitating fatigue, yet her heart raced like she'd just run a marathon. Her mind cycled through an endless loop of scenes: Brandon, Nico's corpse, Anna, Samantha's face skinned clean off. Over and over, these scenes replayed in her head.

Frustrated, she concluded that her efforts to rest were not going to bear any fruit. There was no way she'd be able to fall asleep in this state—not even for a cat nap.

"I can't sleep..."

"Yeah, neither could we. We tried to watch the place in shifts, but neither of us were actually able to fall asleep. It's all just... so much." Shannon said.

Jeanette detected the vulnerability in her voice. This was a good sign.

"Where did you guys come from?"

THEM

"We were in the city," Alex said, "you should've seen it, it was complete chaos. All of this shit just happened overnight. We drove off, but my truck ran out of gas after a few hours. We ditched it and hiked out here."

Shannon interjected, "Look, I'm sorry I jumped you like that."

"I don't blame you. I've seen *them* with my own eyes."

For a brief second there, she detected a half-smile on Shannon's face.

"Hey, thanks for understanding. Look, I made you share your experience, so we might as well share ours. Alex?"

"Yeah, go ahead."

Shannon nodded.

"So, long story short, he and I are together, and we live... uh, *lived*, with this roommate named Rhea. We got home last night, and Rhea still hadn't left her room. We could hear this weird crunching sound, but we didn't think anything of it. She was always quite strange. Anyway, when the emergency broadcast played, we got all spooked... so we checked on her," Shannon turned away, looking into the distance, "the door to her room was unlocked, and she was lying on the floor in a puddle of blood. Her entire sternum was torn open, and this guy was kneeling over her... he was

THEM

eating her organs. So then–"

Shannon's breath hitched.

"Then I grabbed my gun," Alex continued, "I called out to the guy, and he looked at us and... I still don't know if I saw it right, but, like..."

"The man-eating Rhea was... well, Alex. He was wearing Alex's jersey, and he had Alex's exact face."

"Please tell me you killed it." Jeanette says.

"Blasted him clean through the head. We tried to call the cops, but our calls weren't going through."

"Same."

It was clear that Jeanette was in the same boat as them. A slight tingling of reassurance budded inside her at the notion that she wasn't the only one going through this ordeal. The dread hadn't subsided, but she'd be lying if she said that there wasn't that fleeting sensation of catharsis.

"What do you think they are?" Jeanette says, breaking the silence.

"Who's to say? Doppelgangers? Mimics? Clones? It doesn't matter. There's no rational way to explain what's going on."

"Just how bad is it in the city?"

"Shan?" Alex said.

Shannon dug into her rucksack and took out a chunky

THEM

professional camera. Jeanette assumed Shannon had been a photographer before all this. Shannon then handed the camera over to her. This wasn't the city—no, this was a warzone. This was the kind of thing you'd see on the TV. Photographs like this were seen on international news when they showed the most recent country America had bombed under the pretense of world peace.

Jeanette's heart sank as she flimsily handed the camera back.

"I had no idea..."

"I'm sorry you had to see that... but it's the truth of what's going on. I edit documentaries and, one day, I'll have enough footage to make something of this shitty situation."

"Fair enough. And what does he do?" Jeanette tilted her head to Alex.

"I was in law school," Alex started, "but I had to take a leave of absence to help my mom out. She'd been undergoing chemo and we don't have enough to afford a caregiver as it is. In the meantime, I'm working the night shift at the hospital she's at so I can spend time with her."

"I'm so sorry to hear that... is she getting better?"

"Unfortunately not."

THEM

Jeanette was taken aback by the sudden crumbling of Alex's tough exterior. He'd gone from wolf to scared puppy in a matter of seconds. He had the thousand-yard stare of a battle-weary soldier. She decided not to pry him for any more details.

"And you, Jeanette? What was your life like before all this."

"Not much. I lived alone with my blonde Labrador, Nico. He..." she choked back a sob, "he was killed by one of *them* last night."

"Bastards." Shannon spat.

"Other than that, I worked this standard 9-5 sales job as a telemarketer... In other words, I was verbally abused by old white people who wanted nothing to do with me for eight hours a day with a forty-five-minute lunch break."

"I'd clean toilets with my tongue before taking a KPI-based cold calling gig," Shannon said.

"I'm honestly contemplating a career change. I was thinking of trying out so–"

She went silent.

"What was that?"

Metal grated against metal.

It could've come from anywhere, seeing as how buildings with ceilings this high tend to trap sound,

THEM

Jeanette told herself.

"Whatever that was, I don't like it." Alex said.

Shannon made a beeline for the door across the one they walked in.

"I don't like it either. We need to go. Join us?"

The thought of being alone frightened Jeanette, so she elected to join them despite how tired she was. If joining other people meant having to fight off her fatigue just a little bit longer, she'd do it.

Alex pried open the large metal door adjacent to the hallway. Shannon turned on the flashlight of her phone. The inside looked more or less the same. It was a massive room with another series of catwalks and machines. Beyond the room was a long, circular tunnel that led to a flight of stairs down to the boiler room.

"You guys, I found something." Shannon said from across the chamber.

"Is that a passageway?"

Under her was a hatch presumably leading into the ground below the factory. It was sealed shut by a lock and chain. The lock was so rusty Alex managed to kick it free after several tries.

"This must lead to the sewers. We can try to get to the other town through there and hopefully find more survivors."

THEM

Alex forced open the hatch, the hinges squeaked as he heaved up the rusty lid. At last, it gave and fell with a crash. Shannon shined the light into the hole to reveal a ladder. Droplets of water plinked in the recesses of the expanse below them.

"I'll go check it out." Alex said.

He descended the ladder first. A splash sounded as he landed. Shannon and Jeanette then followed. Three inches of water lined the floor. Jeanette's stomach turned as the viscous grime soaked her lacerated foot. She struggled to hold back her vomit as the putrid stench hit her. Her wounds burned as they collided with the gunk coating the floor beneath the water. This would no doubt lead to infection.

I can't afford to dwell on this now, she thought, steadying herself.

Rats squeaked and chattered through the tunnel. A disgusting stench of rot and feces wafted through the underpass. Shannon took the phone out of her pocket and flashed the light ahead of them.

The entire floor came into sight.

Shannon let out an ear-piercing scream.

The passageway was littered with human remains and fungus-infested skeletons. Several of the corpses even seemed to look fresh. There was a dead man, looking

THEM

straight at them. He was calcified with a gaping smile. His irises were indistinguishable from the rest of his eye–the eyeballs were entirely black. Jeanette knew, from sheer instinct alone, that he was one of *them*. But what was the corpse of one of those mimics doing down here?

"I can't... I can't be here." Shannon said.

Alex pulled her into a hug, "We should just turn back."

Jeanette nodded. Alex went ahead and climbed up the ladder. Shannon followed after him, but only got about half way when he came to an abrupt halt. Just then, the faint sound of a cackle echoed.

"Shit, shit!" Alex hissed.

"What?"

"Get down, go."

"Babe, why? I can't be down here, I..."

"Shan, they're fucking everywhere. I don't know how they got in, but the place is full of them. They've got weapons. Fuck, hurry up!"

Shannon begrudgingly sprung back down with a splash. Alex lightly pulled on the lid and shut it, swaddling them in complete darkness once again.

THEM
CHAPTER 6

Above them, a world of daylight awaited—a world that no longer resembled the one they'd been in just under twenty-four hours ago. Just as the sun rose with the promise of a new day, they were forced once again into the cloying night.

Shannon activated the flashlight on her phone, reintroducing them to the festering sight. Jeanette's eyes lingered on the dead man. There was something about his black eyes—something about his lifelessness.

Just then, she could've sworn he blinked.

"You guys, my phone is about to die." Shannon said.

"Fuck. Can you try putting it on low power mode?"

"It's been on low power since last night," she swiped down to check the battery. "Shit! It's on like 7%, this thing will be dead in minutes. Where's your phone?"

"Dead. Do you have any suggestions?"

They needed the phone to reach the outside world should this sewer lead to a place with a signal. Jeanette's mind scrambled for answers. Was there any other source of light that could replace it? She'd dropped her phone, so they were two phones down, but perhaps...

"Shannon, does your camera have a flash?"

THEM

Shannon pushed a few buttons on the camera and then clicked. That one flash lit up the entire cavern even better than the phone. The burst left just as quickly as it came, but that brief nanosecond was enough to give them a snapshot of the place ahead.

"Jeanette, I could fucking kiss you right now."

"Alright, good," Alex sighed in relief. "Let's navigate with this camera flash and get the hell out of here. I'll lead with the camera. Jeanette, hold on to Shan, Shan hold on to me. No one let go; we'll take this slowly."

"I hope we find a place to sit at some point."

"Yeah, please. I'm fucking spent."

"Let's hope somewhere less wet is up ahead."

They linked arms and wriggled forward. The wriggle turned into a shuffle, then into baby steps. They steadily inched onward as Alex flashed their path. Each flash was merely a blink, but it was enough to penetrate the unknown trail up ahead and raise their spirits just enough. They'd pushed steadily for what seemed like hours before Jeanette's legs buckled from her debilitating drowsiness.

With each burst of the camera, it seemed like there was no exit. No matter how long they'd walked, the direct view up ahead still resembled nothing more than a black hole.

THEM

Water splashed back and forth as their feet waded through the fetid marsh of bacteria. The sound was relaxing. It had the same effect as walking along a beach's shoreline at night.

Jeanette pretended she was at a tropical marina and the gritty filth brushing against the soles of her feet was coarse sand.

Jeanette daydreamed of her thirteenth birthday which she spent at Santa Monica pier with her family. The sun's buttery rays cast a warm, gentle hand over her forehead. She stuck out her tongue, recalling how she had guiltlessly lapped up the chocolate shell-coated vanilla ice cream. She tasted the sweetness of the cotton candy, and the savory mustard-soaked hot dogs she'd had for lunch. She salivated as she relished the creamy cheddar spread on toast topped with tomatoes and bacon strips she had that wonderful day. Her stomach groaned as the painful hunger pangs kicked in. She was so thirsty she half considered drinking the filthy water they had been walking in.

"Fuck, can we take a breather?" Shannon said, breaking Jeanette out of her reverie.

My sentiments exactly, Jeanette thought.

"Sure," Alex said.

Unlinking their hands, they took a break to stretch

THEM

and catch their breath. Bones clicked as Shannon keeled over to stretch her worn hamstrings. A loud pop came from Alex craning his neck backward and side to side. Jeanette sank down into a squat to gather herself. Her head had gone light from starvation; if she hadn't taken this time to rest she knew she would've passed out. The sloshing of water ceased; all Jeanette could hear were the sounds of their breaths, and the penetrating ring brought forth by dead silence.

Inhale, exhale–you'll get through this, she remembered her dad telling her whenever she'd cry.

A splash puttered, breaking the silence.

"Hey, don't jump the gun. If you walk ahead of us you'll get lost."

"That wasn't me, I'm right here."

"Jeanette?"

"Here..." She wheezed.

"Are you splashing around down there?"

"N-no, I swear."

"Shan, really?"

"It's not me, what the fuck? You guys this isn't fucking funny."

"I'm not doing anything, I'm–"

A groan, followed by a faint cackle reverberated off the walls. Alex pointed the camera behind them and

THEM

snapped. In that brief flash of light, all three of them gasped. A shadow was crouched on the ground.

Snap.

Out of the water emerged an oily, tar-coated skeleton.

Snap.

"Shannon, get your phone out!"

It steadily craned upward from its slouch and stood about seven feet high. Its limbs cracked with the sound of dry bones grating against one another and snapping. Its jaw was embellished with an assortment of mangled, almond-shaped, razor-sharp teeth.

Snap.

"Fuck!" Shannon cursed.

She finally managed to fire the flash of her phone up ahead.

The creature was gone.

She turned around, only to illuminate Alex's petrified stare. A black, greasy hand gripped his neck. It dragged him down into the black abyss. Jeanette and Shannon ran toward him. The light source shook erratically, illuminating only portions of the cylindrical tunnel.

Frazzled, Jeanette was torn between running in the opposite direction on her own or staying with Shannon. She knew she couldn't possibly outrun the beast. This was no time for quiet contemplation and rational

THEM

thought—she only had one conviction and instinct: fight.

The creature buried its fangs into Alex's thigh. Shannon screamed as Jeanette darted forward, grabbing her knife from Shannon's belt strap. She launched forward and plunged it right into the creature's eye. She yanked the knife out. The suction and popping noise indicated that its yellow eye had come with it. She drew back her arm and thrusted the blade into the demon's face and neck, digging and twisting as it emitted a rattling, cavernous howl. Shannon took her own hunting knife and joined in. Its mewls only satisfied them. They stabbed and stabbed and stabbed, releasing blood-curdling screams. The more damage they inflicted, the more the monster's howl resembled that of a shrill pig in an abattoir. Shannon pointed the barrel of the gun at its head.

"Eat this, motherfucker!"

She pulled the trigger. The barrel blasted at close range. Its head erupted in black globs of clumpy oil. Alex fell from the weakened beast's grasp into the murky waste water. The damage was severe. His leg now had a series of craters oozing chunks of melted black berries and creamy pus.

"Okay, you grab one arm and I'll get the other."

THEM

They looped each of his arms around their shoulders, hauled him up, and continued their trek into the darkness.

Jeanette and Shannon took turns lighting up the passage with the camera. Jeanette took a deep breath to steady her nerves, and then they trudged forward into the endless stretch of tunnel.

The stench was so foul they stung at their eyes like minced onions.

Water sloshed to the right. Shannon snapped the camera, revealing a tunnel adjacent to them. There were intermittent spaces of silence, and then the shuffling of feet and spattering would resume. Jeanette's throat dried up, stealing her breath, and making her heart race. In that brief respite of silence, there were no scurrying roaches or rats. It was easy to let someone's imagination run wild in these dark places.

The air was infused with the musky scent of human waste. Jeanette's lungs burned with how much less eagerly she was inhaling. This was the stench of death with an exponentially concentrated proof.

The ceiling had gradually gotten lower. They ducked their heads as the fungal granite scraped against their scalps. The air thinned. They took gulps of breath, only

THEM

to gag and hack at the foulness of it.

The lack of oxygen merged with the excruciating physical exertion took a toll. Jeanette's knees buckled, her chest ached, the caves containing her eyes throbbed with a dull pain. Claustrophobia seized her every movement. The ceiling wasn't just getting lower, the walls were closing in. None of them could walk upright anymore.

Their excursion was brought to a sudden halt when they ran to a dead end.

"No, no, no! Fuck!" Shannon cried.

"Shan..."

Alex rasped like he'd just run a marathon. If they didn't get to a hospital soon, he would no doubt expire.

"Shannon, try lighting it up."

"Why? We're fucked either way. Fuck... *they* are going to catch up with us aren't they?"

"Shannon, breathe. Please. Stay with me."

"I am fucking breathing!"

"Listen. Inhale, count to five, count to five holding it in, and then exhale for about seven to eight seconds."

"Fuck that."

"Please, just try..." Jeanette's voice croaked.

"Fuck you! You know we're dead and there's nothing we can do. There's a fucking wall in front of us, and if

THEM

we turn back who knows what could be there? We're dead. We're fucking dead!"

"Shan..." Alex said with all the effort he could muster.

The pain in his words must've connected with Shannon. Her sobs calmed. She breathed in despite the snot clogging her nose. She held it in, paused, and eased the restorative breath out through her mouth. She repeated this drill about five more times, breathing in through her nose and out through her mouth.

"Okay..." She said at last.

"Alright, now light up what's above us. I know this echo is coming from somewhere, and it doesn't make sense that there would suddenly be a dead end out of nowhere."

"Right. They must've built it like this for a reason."

"I was thinking the same thing."

Shannon couldn't see it, but—in the darkness—Jeanette smiled at her. She knew what it was like to be inconsolable, to be so despondent, to want nothing more than to quit. But Shannon didn't quit, and this fighting spirit was going to get them through this. Shannon pointed the lens of the camera up at an acute angle and snapped.

Sure enough, the echoes were coming from somewhere. Just a few feet above them was a platform

THEM

that led to higher ground.

"Yes! Let's go."

"Shannon, you and I should get up there, then let's both work to get Alex up."

"Got it."

Shannon and Jeanette climbed up–they each took one of Alex's hands and hoisted him up. He was weak, but he had just enough strength to maneuver himself onto the ledge. Shannon swept the elevated ground with the phone light, finding the source of the fetid stench.

Up ahead was a dead man. He was lying face down.

"What happened to this poor guy?"

His body writhed with a swarm of greedy cockroaches. The man didn't look like he'd been dead for very long. Alex flipped him over and instantly dry-heaved. The man's entire sternum had been pried open, revealing a gaping cavern of tattered entrails. His breastbone had been torn into. His heart and eyes were missing.

What could've done this to him? Could it have been that thing we just killed?

Jeanette felt as if she was at the bottom of the ocean, hopelessly treading toward the surface as her supply of oxygen depleted, yet never able to reach it. The further she swam, the more inefficacious her attempts were for

THEM

all she knew, she had likely just been sinking down to the bottom this entire time.

They glowered, perplexed at the macabre sight before them. He looked like he had been mauled by an animal. There were obviously no large animals down here, yet evidence of some grisly apex predator lay before them. He had been unmade without a single shred of elegance. The entire wall in front of him was splattered with flecks of blood and viscera caked in black, syrupy oil.

"Shannon, point the light there."

Shannon angled the light to the right. Next to them was another narrow stretch of tunnel.

"Should we go?"

"Frankly, I don't see any other option."

"I just hope we're not all out of luck."

They continued down the passage ahead. Shannon scanned the footpath with her flashlight–there was a peculiar absence of rats and cockroaches. Even the water had fallen silent. Jeanette grew nervous.

An echoed cackle splintered the silence.

It wasn't just one laugh; it was a faint series of overlapping laughter. The laughter echoed all over–it was impossible to tell which specific direction it came from.

THEM

Was it behind us? Did it come from up ahead? Should we go back or press forward?

The laugh was inhuman, it was like the strained and piercing cry of a hawk. It grew louder with each passing second. Just then, a low groaning sound barreled through the tunnel, ricocheting off the narrow walls of the waterway.

Every hair on Jeanette's body stood up. Once again, her high-strung imagination took over. She pictured a monster from one of the story books her father had read to her when she was young. Even then, she'd had the rational mind to flippantly dismiss these grisly fairy tales, yet circumstances were now forcing her to grant these intrusive thoughts an air of credence.

She saw ogres with red glowing eyes and monstrous bodies. As they trudged forward, she envisioned these hell beasts waiting for them in one of the adjacent passageways, inching closer and closer toward them. These creatures could see in the darkness. They could sense the warmth in their bodies with thermal vision. They had long, shredded talons that gritted against the mossy granite.

Could I actually hear this?

Is this actually happening?

Scalding moisture pierced the corners of her eyes,

THEM

giving way to tears. Hard as she tried, she couldn't soothe her rapid heart. She couldn't banish the thoughts of this abomination from her mind's eye. The invasive image of death kept flooding back in the more she tried to snuff it. She saw it standing right above them, raising its large, gnarled claw. She felt it moments away from spouting a feral howl right before it buried its talon into her throat.

There's no such things as monsters, right? Right?
There are.
And they look like you and I.

How did she know she could trust Shannon and Alex? How was she so sure they weren't deliberately leading her right toward danger? She prayed that the sound was just her anxious mind playing tricks on her. Her gaze was downcast.

"Fuck!" Shannon screamed.

"What?"

"Another fucking dead end!"

Her entire chest caved in.

"Fuck, fuck, FUCK!"

"Stop," Jeanette wheezed, "you'll lead *them* straight to us!"

"They're already on their way here. We're fucked, I don't want to be around for this."

THEM

Shannon raised the barrel of the gun to her head.

"No! Shannon, think about this, please!"

"Fuck you! Fuck everything!"

"Shan, please!" Alex cried.

"Shut up! Both of you. Just shut up!"

Her entire body quivered under her heavy sobs. Alex tried to grab the gun from her hand, casting all caution to the wind. She shoved him away and pointed the barrel under her jaw.

"I-I beg you, Shan, please don't leave me."

Shannon collapsed to her knees, letting out a massive wail. She fell onto Alex and sank into his shoulder.

"What the fuck is happening..."

"I don't know."

These three words were, perhaps, the most horrific thing Jeanette had ever heard. All her life she'd been a problem solver. She graduated from college with top marks, she got a job, she got her own place while many of the people she'd gone to school with still lived in flatshares.

But this? Now? She didn't have the first clue what to do next. She had a singular goal: survive. But she had no plan. She yanked Shannon's phone and scanned the room with the flashlight to gather her bearings.

I guess it's finally time to admit that I am completely

THEM

fucking lost.

She pointed the flashlight up in hopes of finding a ladder, yet she was met only with copper pipes and peeling insulation running across the ceiling. Every surface was dotted with filth and debris. The dark, silent tunnel yielded no answers. In the midst of her inspection, she backed up against the tunnel wall.

Her heel struck a metal surface.

The shock almost knocked her breathless.

Jeanette inspected the source, alarmed and curious. There was a metal latch in the ground that blended into the mold and grime. She tugged the latch sideways and pulled on the metal lid. Pointing the flashlight into the pit, she noticed bars of corroded metal.

A ladder.

This discovery was met with another round of ear-piercing cackles.

"Guys, down here!"

"What?"

"A ladder. Let's go. Now!"

Shannon was all out of options, so she nodded. Jeanette went first, Shannon second. Alex held on tight, then dropped onto both their arms. He fell with a thud, but they'd managed to break his fall just enough to prevent any serious injuries.

THEM

They took this as their chance and bolted forward into the darkness. They trudged forward without a thought or caring of where they were going.

Jeanette's bowels lurched. Shannon swung her flashlight this way and that. She had an arduous time catching enough breath. Her mouth was parched. Her heart slammed. Her face dripped with thick, sour sweat. Her soaked hair was plastered to her cheeks and forehead. Her blouse clung to her skin, soaked with perspiration. The tunnel's dense heat was so overbearing she felt like she was being cooked inside her own clothes.

Something tickled her underneath her blouse, just above her stomach.

Have the cockroaches come back?

Wasting no time, she slapped herself as the insect scampered up to her chest. She finally caught it, feeling it crumble and squish. It pulped into the moisture of her sweat, stuck to her with its own juices.

Her neck was stiff, her head splitting, her blood vessels wheezed, her bladder filled to the brim. Her lungs seared with fire as she was not used to this type of intense physical activity. Sweat stung her eyes. Yet she pushed, to get away from both *them* and the monsters in her head.

THEM

Just then, like divine intervention, a beacon of light glinted in the dark horizon. It was a gray, jagged beam rippling into the water like a thin glowing pole in the distance.

"Up ahead!"

"I see it," Alex said, gasping for air between words.

Once again, the ground began to meet the ceiling with each passing step. There was a pattern of light on the floor because, in the far end, there was a grate. Behind them, they heard that same banshee howl of a cackle growing stronger. The metal grate was at the far end of a narrow crawl space. Jeanette went first, Shannon went behind her, and Alex held onto Shannon's legs. They inched forward, granite and fetid liquid grime scraped at their elbows and forearms. The walls closed in, raking Jeanette's scalp and bare shoulders.

Jeanette shoved at the grate. It didn't budge. She pushed at it again, only to yield the same result. She took the knife and dug it into the corner, chipping away at the rust that had baked itself into the granite. The rusted iron tore against her skin as she punched at it. Her knuckles split, caking her fists with globules of thick blood. The maniacal laughs got so loud they were practically in earshot.

"Weeee gotcha!"

THEM

Alex started screaming. The sound of his terror merged with the sound of tearing fabric.

"Help! Help! Oh gahh..."

"Jeanette hurry the fuck up!!!"

"I'm fucking trying!"

"Hold on to me, baby. Don't let go!" Shannon screamed for dear life.

Steeling her breath, her heart raced as heat surged through her entire body. She shoved the grate with both hands now, moving so frantically that she bashed her head on the hard cement above. The pain slammed down through her body. Her vision flashed. Her heart galloped. Her bowels turned to water as the sound of gurgling vomit came from behind her.

At last, the grate began to budge.

"Fucking hurry up, they're killing him!" Shannon screamed.

And with one last mighty roar, Jeanette pushed the grate with everything she had.

The cold light of dawn burned her eyes as she hauled herself out, landing on her face. She shifted onto her back, soaking in the vast, open sky.

It was a gray morning, the sky was overcast, and a light drizzle fell upon her. She hauled herself up to help Shannon pull Alex out. His skin was as pale as the sky

THEM

above them. Lines of blood spilled out of his mouth. His hand was limp in Jeanette's.

"Let go, you mother fuckers!"

"Shannon, put your foot against the wall like me. We need to force him out."

Shannon gritted her teeth, pressed the sole of her foot against the slippery cement, and pushed with all her might. Alex finally gave and slid out.

Jeanette's heart stopped when she saw what had become of him. His entrails hung out of him like fleshy tendrils of mangled vines. His lower torso looked like a botched cesarean.

A jolt surged through Jeanette as a blast erupted next to her ear.

Shannon fired her pistol at one of the laughers crawling out of the narrow tunnel. She shot at his face again and again. Dots of bullet holes proliferated all over his head, turning him into fleshy Swiss cheese.

His mangled face was locked in that demonic, Cheshire grin.

"Fuck you! Fuck you all to hell!"

Shannon shot into the hole and screamed. When she lowered the gun, Jeanette rushed forward, lifted the grate to the hole, and kicked it into place.

Cackles bellowed from the pit.

THEM

Past the dead one, there was a constellation of glowing eyes that reminded her of the monsters in her dream; that reinforced that these monsters were real.

Behind her, Shannon sobbed. Her face was so red, and her cries were so loud it almost looked as if she was going to start weeping tears of blood. Next to her, Alex was completely destroyed. It took everything in Jeanette to hold back her vomit. Alex's chest pulsed as he coughed geysers of blood. His exposed, crystalline organs still beat with life. The musky smell of shit invaded Jeanette's nose—she knew Alex had no chance.

Shannon was on all-fours, touching her forehead to his as she screamed. She bawled her eyes out and beat the ground with her fists.

"No, baby, no! Don't leave me! You promised you'd never let me go. Please. Please stay with me!!"

Jeanette's eyes burned with tiredness. She slumped to the ground, realizing that she'd been awake and active for over thirty-six hours. All she wanted to do after the grueling work week was rest, yet here she was—fighting for her life with her dwindling energy. She wanted to lie down and sleep. She wanted to close her eyes, wake up in bed, and discover that all of this had just been one sick nightmare.

She instead glared at the sky with fury.

THEM
CHAPTER 7

As far as she could see, the swath of land in front of her was desolate. There was nothing more than a handful of houses and cars. A couple of cars had been completely totaled into one another. This place is empty now, but it hasn't always been like this.

Something flew at her leg.

She looked down and saw that it was a stray paper of a missing cat with an emergency contact number to call should it be found.

Down the road were a series of restaurants and buildings. The windows were broken. It looked like total chaos had broken out here not long ago. She walked into the misty street and saw several bodies lying down sideways.

Could it be *them?* Could it be homeless people who'd escaped all the carnage?

If it had been any other day, the wide-open space would've been soothing. Now, all she could think of was how *they* could pounce out of anywhere. Impending danger could suddenly materialize out of nowhere and kill her with its bare hands. Shannon's hysterical sobs weren't doing them any favors. Her high-pitched wails stood out like a flare amidst an open sea.

THEM

"Shannon, please try and keep it down."

"Fuck you! Just fuck off!"

Jeanette had had enough of her abuse; she had half the mind to leave her and just let *them* take care of her. Yet Shannon was the one who was armed with the gun and Jeanette highly doubted she'd willingly surrender it.

"No, fuck you!" Jeanette yelled, shocking herself, "do you wanna fucking die out here, huh? Do you think that's what Alex would want? You stupid fucking bitch cunt!"

Shannon looked at her with a pained expression. She opened her mouth to say something, but no words came out. Instead, her face crumpled as more tears welled in her eyes. She cried silently now, turning her gaze away from Alex.

Alex had a glazed, empty look in his eyes. They were vacant and lifeless. His chest no longer moved.

Alex was gone.

The look in his deceased eyes reminded Jeanette of *their* eyes. The thought chilled every sinew down to her bone.

Shannon bit into her bottom lip as she cried into her dirty palms. Her back heaved up and down as she bent forward, curling into a ball on the cold, wet road.

THEM

The light drizzle turned into a modest shower. It cascaded over them as they remained in their positions. Conviction seized Jeanette at that moment.

"Wait here."

She gripped the handle of the butcher knife in her bloody hand and trudged forward. She started toward one of the motionless bodies lying by a nearby gutter. With her foot, she flipped him onto his back. The man's eyes had been gouged out. His sternum had been cracked open, and all his innards had been unspooled. Under him lay a fresh stream of crimson flowing with the rainwater into the gutter.

"Hey," Shannon said.

Jeanette faced her. Shannon's arms were crossed, her head was still tilted down. Her body trembled under the freezing drops of rain.

"Hey."

"Look, I'm... I'm sorry. I didn't mean to curse you out. I... I just–"

"Don't mention it, Shannon."

Jeanette gently eased Shannon into a hug. Shannon buried her head into Jeanette's shoulder and whimpered once again. She was an absolute mess, but she couldn't be blamed. If they'd just found the exit a few minutes earlier, Alex would have been standing

THEM

next to them now. His presence provided both of them with a sense of security. He was a chiseled six-foot tall man who would've protected Shannon at any cost. And now they only had each other.

"I miss him, Jeanette. I miss him so fucking much already. I don't know how I'm going to go on... I'm so fucking lost."

"I've got you, Shannon. I won't let go."

Shannon returned the embrace, holding on to Jeanette like they were lost at sea, and she was the only means of buoyancy. Their transient moment of comfort was interrupted by faint cackles; the shrill, pestering sound of a robin's screech above the tenors. There was no doubt that it was ways away, but it still sent a current of electricity up Jeanette's spine.

"We should get a move on."

"Yeah..."

"I'm starting to see a pattern with how *they* kill us. It's like they want to excavate everything that makes us... us."

"I think I know what you mean..."

Jeanette took Shannon's hand. As they walked along a long stretch of pavement, mist hovered over the road like a blanket of clouds. They hastened their steps, broken glass crunched under shoes like snapping

THEM

crackers.

"I think the gun's out of ammo."

"We'll figure it out, just stay close."

Jeanette's every move had gone so lethargic it was as if someone had released noxious poison in the air to numb her muscles. Despite being out in the open, the air still reeked with a musty stench. There were no visual indications of life. No movement–just stillness.

Despite covering a decent amount of ground on their trek, Jeanette's mind was still stuck in that hellish thought loop. The sky brightened as the minutes elapsed, yet the sun was still obscured by the clouds and fog.

There was an unmistakable sound of feet scraping against concrete. This came with a millisecond of relief as Jeanette imagined that they'd be rescued and taken in by a ragtag band of survivors. Then it hit her, *they* looked just like us–there's no way she'd be able to tell who she could and couldn't trust.

Her body went numb with dread.

Her first instinct was to sprint, but her legs spurned in defiance. The dense mist obstructed her view of the path ahead. The dull thud of footsteps grew more tumultuous. Shannon's gaze was still downcast. Jeanette ripped the gun out of Shannon's hands and

THEM

pointed it to the sky and fired two rounds.

"Come at me, you motherfuckers! I dare you. I fucking dare you!"

The sound of feet skidded across the pavement like raccoons tearing through a thick shrub. These noises ran above one another indicating that there were several sources. The sound came and went, generating frequencies from all directions. Jeanette's stomach clenched in fright.

I think we're surrounded.

"Shannon. We need to run."

Shannon nodded. The two broke out into a grueling sprint, pushing past their anxiety and exhaustion. The adrenaline had woken them up and given them a second wind. They tore through the street, hands linked, hearts racing. Jeanette wanted to put as much distance between herself and those things as she could.

Those things that looked like people.

Those things that looked like *them*.

After running for what felt like a few miles, her mind started to form coherent thoughts once again.

Where did they come from? Are they interdimensional beings from another planet? Did someone, somewhere, open a portal to hell? Why do they look like carbon copies of us?

THEM

A sudden grumble in her stomach interrupted her stream of contemplation. Hunger pangs punched through her gut again. A thudding ache built at her temples and between both her eyes. She wasn't just terribly sleep deprived—she was also starving. She needed food, and she needed it as soon as humanly possible. She could no longer sprint, so she slowed down.

"Hey, I'm... I'm fucking spent." Jeanette wheezed.

"Same. What do you suggest?"

"It feels like we've been running in circles. I think we need to stop for a bit to regroup and find out where we are."

"I-I don't know about that."

"Please. I think I'm about to pass out. I can't go on for much longer. I need to eat something."

"Jeanette..."

"Come on, Shannon... We need some energy; we need to charge our batteries."

"I-I don't have any money on me... I've only got a few quarters."

"We're not going to need any money," Jeanette said, brandishing her butcher knife.

"What are you saying? We're not going to kill innocent people, are we?"

THEM

Jeanette stood motionless as she weighed what had just come out of her mouth. It was strange to be in this mindset–the one that prioritized survival over ethics. It made her feel powerful, but at what cost? It would be great, she thought, if she could just un-learn all the morals and principles she'd been raised with. Where would they get her in a world like this? She wondered if being as ruthless as *them* was what it took to survive in a godforsaken hellscape such as this.

"Yeah, Shannon. If it comes to it."

"No."

"Then let me ask you this: how the fuck do you know whose innocent anymore? I don't know if all this is going on all over the world, or if it's just here. What I do know is that *they* don't play by the same rules. Do you want to survive this, or not?"

Shannon exhaled a long, shivering breath from her mouth.

"I can't."

"Yes, you can. I'm going to gut the next person that tries us, and you're going to shoot them."

"What is this? Why the fuck is all this happening?" Shannon whimpered.

"I don't know."

Quickly, she scanned the side of the town they'd run

THEM

to. She spotted a few small cafes, buildings, and a gas station. She could practically taste the familiar bitterness of gas station coffee and the sweetness of warm honey glazed doughnuts. The thought alone was enough to turn her cravings feral.

"Over there, the gas station."

Shannon followed her into the parking lot which led to the convenience store. Something a few paces ahead seized Jeanette's attention.

"Hey, you said you had a few quarters, right?"

"Yeah... why?"

"There's a payphone up there by the pumps. I need to check on my dad, please. He's all I have left."

Shannon frowned, clearly sensing the desperation in her voice. She dug into her front pocket and handed Jeanette all the money she had left. Jeanette took the money and pulled Shannon into a tight hug, nuzzling her face into the side of Shannon's head. She gave her a light kiss on the cheek as she fought back tears.

"Thank you," she whispered.

Jeanette jammed the quarters into the slot, one after the other, and used her finger to stab the buttons of her dad's number. She waited.

Ring.

Ring.

THEM

Ring.

Ring.

Ring.

Someone finally picked up. They said nothing.

"Dad? Dad?!"

"W-who is this?"

"Dad! It's me, Jeanette," she sighed with relief, still perturbed by the belligerent tone in his voice.

"Jeanette? What kind of sick fucking joke is this?"

Her heart skidded in her chest.

"What? Dad, it's me. What's going on? Are you and Janice okay?"

Why is he being so hostile? What have I done to deserve this treatment? Even when he'd raised his voice at me as a child, he'd never taken this tone with me, let alone use profanity. The man I know as my loving father is unrecognizable now...

"You're sick, whoever you are."

"Dad, it's Jeanette. Jeanette! Your daughter! I know this isn't my number, I'm calling you on a payphone, I'm—"

"That's impossible, and I don't appreciate this shit you're trying to pull. My daughter is with me right now, sitting in the living room. She's been here for over an hour. I don't know what game you think you're

THEM

playing–"

Jeanette's entire universe came to a sudden stop.

"Dad! No no no that's not her–err, me! I don't know what they are. It's a double. It's not human, dad. Dad!"

"Just listen to yourself, you fucking crazy bitch! Fuck you for wasting my time. I am done with you. I am hanging up now."

"Dad, wait. No! Dad Plea—"

The busy tone beeped before she could finish that last sentence. Had someone gone through all the contacts on her phone and tracked her father down, trying to replicate her appearance? What did *they* actually look like? What did they want? Where did they come from?

"Fuck!" Jeanette screamed, kicking the road.

"Fuck, fuck, fuck!"

"Jeanette, what's wrong? What happened?"

Jeanette's heart slammed like a door being kicked shut. The blow of what she'd just learned had sent shockwaves to her spine and into her head. The adrenaline turned into a panic. She suddenly became hyper-aware of all the torment her body had been put through. She felt the crosshatch of welts and scrapes, the gouged abrasions, and the filth coating most of her. The disgust and pain made her muscles watery. Her eyes were like sandpaper behind her eyelids. She

THEM

looked at Shannon and tried to swallow, but it felt like blades had been embedded in her vocal cords. Her teeth clamped shut and chattered–hot pain seared her gums.

"One of *them*..." Her voice trembled.

"Jeanette..."

"One of them got to my dad. I-I tried to tell him," she coughed, "I... he wasn't fucking listening to me. Shannon, we need to go to him. We..." She broke down into a full-fledged wail before she could finish her thought.

"What do you mean, *we*, Jeanette?"

"You're not going to come with me? We can kill that thing and hide out at his place. Shannon, come on..."

Shannon had no words; all she did was cross her arms and glare at the floor.

"Oh fuck... Alright, let's grab some supplies," Shannon said, "we need to hurry, if one of them really is with your dad, we're going to need all the strength and energy to fight this thing off."

"No, I need to go now Shan–"

Jeanette was interrupted by the painful grumbling in her stomach. She'd barely had any dinner last night– this was on top of the fact that she'd gotten no sleep and had yet to mentally process all these events. It felt

THEM

like she'd been stabbed right in her center and the assailant slowly twisted a sword into her. She heaved and coughed. Keeling over, she tried to force out the vomit, only to cough up a bitter wad of bile and mucus.

Looking up, she nearly jumped out of her skin when she saw two versions of Shannon. She backed away, only for both of the Shannon-things to fuse back into one. She'd thought it was a mimic, but it was just her light-headed state. There was no way she'd be able to make it to her dad's place in this state.

Humbled by her fatigue, she relented.

"Alright. But let's make it quick."

THEM
CHAPTER 8

Jeanette stepped in closer to the shop's window, bent over, and cupped her hands to the dark glass. Inside the dim space was the standard row of shelves. Everything stood motionless against the pale dawn light from the overcast sky. She scanned the room from left to right, paranoid that one of *them* would be lurking in the shadows. From what she could tell, the place had been completely ransacked.

"Is it empty?" Shannon said.

"I think so."

"Alright, let's go."

Shannon took her hand as Jeanette pushed open the door. A bell chimed, reverberating off the walls and shelves. Plastic and foil debris crunched under their feet like crispy autumn leaves. The fog from outside had seeped into the door with them. They slowly inched closer into the silent maw of this abandoned outpost.

The lights were switched off, but there had been enough illumination from the outside for them to visually grasp the general area. It was dead silent, save for the ticking of the clock. The road outside was empty, and the feeling of isolation intermingling with aching anticipation was palpable.

THEM

They split up and scanned the shelves, looking for anything to eat. Jeanette found a couple of protein bars and tore into them immediately. Her throat was parched beyond belief, which made swallowing the crunchy treat a painful and laborious task. When she finally managed to put that small bite down, her stomach jumped and gurgled. All she tasted were the sweet oats and the saltiness from the sweat on her upper lip. She had a few beads of sweat off her lip, but her tongue was so dry, and the saltiness made it worse.

"Shannon, do you see anything to drink?"

Shannon shook her head.

"I'll check the back."

"I'm coming with you."

She clicked to open the flashlight, then turned the doorknob to the backroom to the right. The click of the door knob was met with the thrumming sound of rubber skidding along the cement. The sonorous whir of an engine sent shivers down her spine.

The glowing beams of headlights cast away the shadows in front of them. The sudden rap at the front door turned into furious pounding. The headlights were gone, and for a moment, she thought that it had all been in her head. This was until she saw the shell-shocked look on Shannon's face.

THEM

"Shannon, was that a fucking..."

"Car."

"We need to hide. Now." Jeanette whispered.

"Yeah, in here..."

Jeanette feebly laced her fingers around the door's steel bar and pulled. The grating sound of rusted metal bounced off all the walls. If anyone else was here, this surely would have alerted *them*. As they slipped behind the door to the staff room, Jeanette saw three hulking figures standing in the parking lot. They were too tall and brawny to be women. They seemed to be interacting with one another—one of them waved their hands frantically in the air. For a second, she had a glimmer of hope that they were fellow survivors, but she refused to let herself place her trust in them. She shut the door, thrusting herself back into a world of darkness.

"Do you think they're going to try to get in?" Shannon whispered.

"I... Maybe. I hope not."

"Did you see anything? Could you tell who they were?"

"There were about three of them. Probably men."

"Fuck."

"Yeah..."

THEM

"Could they maybe be here to save us? I mean, there's no one left in this town. I don't know why *they* would be here. What would they want?"

The conversation was cut short by the sound of a tray of metal hitting the plastic floor. Jeanette shivered and reached out for Shannon. She felt Shannon's finger and then gripped her hand. Shannon trembled. Gone was the Shannon who held her at knifepoint just hours ago. That Shannon was long dead–this woman was a husk of her former self.

"Jeanette... please tell me you made that sound."

"I... I didn't bump into anything."

"Neither did I, should we–"

They were interrupted once more, this time by a juicy crunch of leather being torn. A popping sound was followed by a gelatinous squishing, punctuated by more tearing.

"Jeanette..."

"Hurry up, turn on your flashlight."

The egg-shaped light shone across the stretch of room. After a few seconds, their eyes adjusted to the sudden brightness. In the far corner of the storage room was a woman hunched over. They were unsure as to what she was doing, all they could gleam from this was the crunching sound of snapping sticks she

THEM

produced. There was a meaty tear, followed by the loud snap and pop of joints being dislodged. The clicks made way for a chorus of gelatinous squishing of rubbery matter.

"Hey..." Shannon said, incredulously.

The woman's back straightened, her head slowly turned to face them. Her irises swam in sicky yellow soup. Her gaze was completely vacant. Her entire front was caked with deep red stains. Beneath her was a man's corpse that had been completely ravaged. There was a ragged hole in his throat that reminded Jeanette of an infant's toothless mouth. Entrails spilled out of him in pink tubes that flopped around in the woman's hands like noodles boiling in water. She mashed the unspooled tubes of intestines in her hands and sucked them into her mouth like she hadn't eaten in years. The oil-slicked entrails ran through her fingers as she munched into them. Doughy globs of semi-digested matter dropped to the floor in gaudy splats.

Shannon's eyes burned in terror. As the woman propped herself up, she puckered his lips and looked straight at Jeanette. Her tongue darted in and out of her mouth as she made slurping and kissing noises at them.

"Tasty, tasty. Death is tasty... Yum-yum." The woman

THEM

rasped.

Red globs squelched through the gaps of her teeth. She licked the black bloodstains on her lips as she lasciviously flicked her tongue up and down.

She then dug her fingers into the man's skull and excavated his eyeball with a popping sound. She bit into the center; gray sludge vomited out at the points her yellowed teeth punctured. She sucked the eyeball into her mouth and chewed, deliberately smacking her lips, and accentuating every wet masticating sound. She then pried open his jaw–angled it in such a way that he could straighten her dominant arm–and popped his jaw loose. The jaw hung limply, supported by paper-thin flesh that had already begun to tear. She leaned in for what seemed like a tender kiss, only to bite the man's tongue and relieve his shattered jaw of it with a meaty rip.

"What do we do..." Jeanette whispered.

"We should make a break for it."

"Shannon..."

The crazed woman glared at them. The smile. Except it wasn't quite a smile. It was her baring her teeth. It was a vile display of bloody, piss-stained enamel with bits of flesh stitched between the gaps. The woman came out of a crouch, then turned to face the beam of

THEM

their flashlight. Her feet were planted squarely in a pool of innards that had once belonged to a person.

And then her face was ten.... Five...two inches away from Jeanette's.

Jeanette had no idea how she managed to lunge at her so quickly, but before she could even take in her next breath, the woman had pinned her to the metal shelf. Empty boxes fell here and there–her hands pawed at Jeanette's crotch and breasts as she licked her chest and throat. Jeanette geared up, ready to release a scream from the inferno of her core.

Bang!

When Jeanette opened her eyes, the woman stared at her. This time, she did so with a black circle on his forehead–smoke wafted out of the deep pit.

The bullet had found its mark.

Blood pulsed out of the crater as if it were a hole in a filled barrel of wine. The woman fell to her knees, and then slowly collapsed backwards like a tree that had just been axed down. Jeanette craned her head to the side. Shannon had unbridled fury in her eyes. She he had her arms extended in front of her, and the gun pointed straight out.

"Fuck... you..." She hissed through gritted teeth.

"I-I thought we were all out?" Jeanette said.

THEM

"Guess not."

"What do we do now?"

Jeanette leaned against the door like she was listening to the inside of a large shell. It was faint white noise—no crinkling of papers, no crunch of broken glass, no sudden footfalls. A sliver of light cast a dull brightness into the storage room as the door creaked open.

Debris and plastic crunched under them once again as they inched closer to the exit. Jeanette held her knife out, gripping it so tight that her knuckles lightened to a shade of soft marble. Shannon pointed her gun out in front of her. They both knew the firearm was empty, but this was done for added effect.

"Where are we going?"

"I think we should look at some of those cars outside and see if any of them still have their keys in them?"

"Then what?"

"I was thinking we could drive to my dad's place and save him from that thing posing as me."

"I don't think that's such a good idea." Shannon said, incredulously.

"I have to try. You can take the car and go wherever you need to; I just need to be with my dad, Shan."

"Jeanette, I don't think I can do this without you..." her voice cracked, "I don't have anyone left. If you died,

THEM

I don't know how I'd..."

Shannon's speech was silenced by a loud thud of metal hitting the floor.

Jeanette turned around.

Shannon's eyes were paralyzed in fear.

Her head was being held close to the chest of a burly man who clamped a hand over her mouth and nose. Her gun lay by her blood-stained shoes. And then Jeanette's feet went out from under her, sending her reeling to the floor. She landed on her tailbone and upper back. All the air in her chest had been slammed out of her. A young man, hiding behind one of the shelves, dug his meaty fingers so tight into her ankle that just a slight increase in pressure could snap it from the joint.

We've been ambushed.

The trance of fear was broken by Shannon's loud shriek as the hefty man shifted her into a sort of headlock.

"Here's some sweet pussy for ya' boy!" he said, as he licked the side of her face.

The other man worked his way up to Jeanette and grabbed a fistful of her hair, smelling it.

"We're going to have loads of fun, toots. First, Imma fuck ya with that there gun! Imma make ya cum nice

THEM

and hard, 'fore I stab ya ta death!"

Without giving it a second thought, Jeanette squared her stance and raised her knee as high as she could. Her kneecap made direct contact with the man's groin, and he released his grip on her. She dashed to the side, grabbed Shannon's fallen gun, and pointed it at her assailant.

"No, no, wait we just wanted to scare yous a little," he laughed, "jeez, you didn't think we was actually gonna hurt you, right?"

"Not so tough now that I can blow your fucking brains out, huh?" Jeanette hissed.

"Look, lady we didn't mean nothing, I swear. My son just likes to play rough games is all."

"Let her go."

"I'm just hugging her, ma'am..." he said, squeezing Shannon's breast.

"I said... Let. Her. Go."

The man reluctantly unhooked his hand from Shannon's jaw, as she fell on all fours and gasped for air.

"Shoot... him..." Shannon croaked.

Jeanette raised the gun at the man who'd accosted Shannon and placed her finger on the trigger...

"No, no wait—that wasn't. Listen miss, I—"

THEM

...and squeezed.

Click.

"No..." Jeanette said as all the blood drained from her face as she came to the realization that the gun was, in fact, empty. Shannon's face was frozen in fear.

Click.

Click.

Click. Click. Click. Click. Click.

And then she was sent to the ground with a harsh blow to the back of her head.

Jeanette prepared to scream, but it was cut short when the burly man's hand clamped over her mouth.

"Don't cry, baby," he growled. "My boys gonna make you feel real good."

"Damn right we are—we are gonna make cum-burping gutter sluts out of these two bitches!"

He pushed Shannon toward Jeanette. The man released Jeanette and shoved her toward a trembling Shannon. The two men closed in on them as Shannon leaned on Jeanette.

"Isaac, take out your switchblade."

With a *snap*, the metal weapon was held up in Jeanette's face. He then grabbed Jeanette by the hair and yanked her head back, craning it so hard her neck cramped. He leaned in, a mere inch from her face. His

THEM

breath smelled like garlic and sun-dried cow hide.

"Now listen here, miss, and listen well. I'm gonna give you and yer little friend some instructions now, and you're gonna follow 'em. No questions asked."

Shannon winced as the younger man grabbed her by the throat.

"Alright blondie, if you don't do exactly as you're told, daddy is gonna make that ugly ginger bitch bleed. Got that?"

She whimpered.

"I said, *got that*?!"

Shannon nodded strenuously as the man tightened his grip on her neck. Her face pinkened, the capillaries in her eyes bulged red. He released her—she sucked in air and coughed.

"Alright, Firecrotch. Lie down."

All Jeanette could do was comply. She got on her knees, propped herself on the floor with her right hand, and slid down onto the plastic wrappers and broken glass. The detritus stabbed at her, but she wasn't about to attempt to take them on. Even she knew her limits. She was willing to do anything to prolong their life. She refused to believe that this was it for her.

"Alright, bimbo. Take your pants off."

Shannon hugged herself and stared at the floor,

THEM

shaking even harder now.

"Listen to me you dumb bitch, I'm talking to you!"

He whacked her on the back of the head, making her hunch forward with a shriek.

"I'm not gonna tell you again, bitch."

Shannon unbuttoned her pants and slid them down to her feet. She kicked the sweatpants to the side and stood there, covering her bruised legs with her hands.

"All of it, you shit-for-brains cunt."

Shannon snapped at him, "fuck you, you sick son of a b–"

Jeanette screamed, interrupting Shannon's protests as the switchblade drew a red line along her right breast. The older man then slapped the side of Jeanette's face so hard the hearing in her ear momentarily blanked into white noise.

"Okay, okay! Sorry..." Shannon said, slipping her underwear off.

"Sheee-yit, oh yeah take em' off."

"Doesn't she have the loveliest legs."

"She'd got a nice firm ass too."

The man yanked the panty out of Shannon's hand and brought it to his noise, sniffing it so hard he snorted.

"Enjoy it all ya want son, this bitch ain't gonna stop ya."

THEM

"Daddy that smells fuckin' good. What's next?"

"Fuck, it's your birthday, boy. Make the call."

He smiled, exposing his rotten gap-toothed grin, and directed his eyes to Jeanette. He pointed the switchblade at Shannon, "alright blondie, get on your knees and straddle her face."

"I... I can't"

"You can't, or you won't? You'll do it either way. You need to choose if you'll do it now, or if you'll do it when your friend is missing her left tit."

"Alright...alright..."

She sagged, kneeled down, and propped herself on top of Jeanette's face.

"Piss on her."

"What?"

"Did I fucking stutter?"

"Y-You can't expect me to piss on command. What the fuck?"

"Need any help?"

"What could you possibly d–"

Before she could finish, the man slugged Shannon in the gut, forcing pungent amber fluid to squirt out of her. It trickled on Jeanette's face, puddling under her head.

"Now slurp that puddle of piss off the floor. Don't you

THEM

dare swallow."

Utterly humiliated, Shannon bent over, propped head up with her hands and slurped up the musky yellow puddle. The piss was stained by the skid marks of shoes—it was clear that the ground hadn't been mopped in days. She gagged and retched but managed to keep the vile liquid in her throat.

"Alright, now lean on top of her and kiss,"

Shannon shook her head, her eyes pleaded for any semblance of compassion.

Jeanette gently brought Shannon's face down and guided her forehead to hers. She hushed her gently. She lightly kissed a teardrop on Shannon's cheek and swiped the other one away with her thumb.

"Shan, it's just us. Don't mind them. We need to keep living, for Alex's sake. We need to get through this."

Shannon shut her eyes and shook her head harder.

"Think about something else... someone else. Close your eyes," Jeanette whispered.

Shannon leaned in and kissed her. Jeanette tried to implement her own advice and imagine someone else, but she couldn't. Who would she imagine? Brandon? He was the only person she'd been intimate with and her memory of him had been tainted. And who would Shannon think of? Alex? The love of her life had just

THEM

been savagely murdered in front of her very eyes. How much more pain was the universe going to inflict on this poor woman?

"Firecrotch, drink the piss out of blondie's mouth."

Jeanette parted her lips and accepted the sour liquid. She tried to swallow it as fast as she could, but there was no way she could mentally bypass the concentrated, bitter aftertaste. She gagged and hacked–bile lurched up her stomach. She could taste her body producing more saliva to line her esophageal passageway. Then, she raised herself up to vomit. The acidic upchuck burned her throat as she forced it out of her gullet.

"Look at the mess y'all made! I want to see yawls clean it up with your mouths. On your knees like the good little sluts you are."

Jeanette dug her fingernails so hard into the palms of her hands that fire shot from her wrists to her elbow. She wedged herself against Shannon as the two of them climbed to their knees. She took a deep breath, mentally preparing herself for what she was about to do. A hand grabbed a fistful of her hair–her face collided with the puke-stained floor so hard a jolt of electricity spiked through her nasal cavity.

"I said eat it, you fucking bitch!"

THEM

Isaac clenched his hand behind her head, thrusting her face into the puddle of vomit. The stomach juices soaked her hair and went up her nose and past her defiant lips. It was a miracle her tooth didn't chip at the force her head whacked against the liquid sick-stained ground. Beside her, Shannon licked at the vile upchuck like a scavenging bird.

Isaac pulled her head up. Blood dripped down her splintered nose. She tilted her head forward so as not to choke on the iron-tasting drip at the back of her throat.

"A'ight. Now I want the two of you to get all hot and heavy, and don't fucking make me say it twice.."

Wasting no time, Shannon unbuttoned Jeanette's blouse and kissed her nipple. She licked the areola, rotating her tongue around the stiffening bud as she intermittently suckled on it.

"Yeah, play with it just like that. That's so fuckin' hot, daddy. Best birthday surprise ever!"

Jeanette felt exposed as the unwelcome air crawled over her pebbled flesh. Through her clouded gaze, she saw the two men leer at them. One licked his lips as the other rubbed at the bulge in his crotch. Their eyes glowed with elation.

The older man then yanked Shannon's head backward and pulled her onto her bum.

THEM

"Spread em' nice and wide."

The other man then grabbed Jeanette and positioned her head in front of Shannon's crotch.

"Come on, you know what to do," he said, pushing Jeanette's face in between Shannon's legs.

"Get her wet. Spit on it."

And so she did. Jeanette had detached herself from her body. As far as she was concerned, she was a bystander lurking in the corner of the convenience store, watching these two women be tormented by these monsters. She was unable to mentally process that she was a participant in these lewd acts of vile degradation.

"Come on, use your tongue to play with her pretty pink slit."

Jeanette squeezed her eyes shut as her tongue made contact with Shannon's dry flesh. She slid her tongue up and down the slit, pretending she was licking an ice cream cone; pretending that she wasn't currently an active participant in the violation of a traumatized, innocent woman.

"Alright, I wanna play now," Isaac said, balling his fist into Jeanette's sweat-slicked hair.

He tackled Jeanette to the ground and straddled her. He pinned both her hands above her head and punched

THEM

her in the face. He rained more blow after blow to her cheek, nose, and chest. The crunching of cartilage cracked and splotched with each hefty blow. He lowered his bloody hand to the inside of her panties and scraped at the tender folds of her labia. He wormed his crusty, dirt-caked fingers into her tight, dry hole as she winced in pain.

"Man, this bitch could really use a wax! Hairy and crusty."

"Easy, son. Ain't that no way to talk to a lady," he said, mockingly.

Jeanette bucked upward in sync with Shannon's screams, but it was no use. He was too heavy and strong to be retaliated against. He purged and spat a custard loogie onto his fingers and buried them, once again, into Jeanette's crotch. He inserted several more fingers, violating her–gyrating his contaminated fist into her pelvis.

"I raised my boys to treat a lady right. It's his sixteenth birthday and—hoo-wee!—are we gon' be celebrating too-day!"

Jeanette's face burned with shame, and her eyes welled with tears. Her bruised ego and humiliation was enough to stiffen Isaac's cock into a robust rod. He thrusted his crotch into the tightness of his jeans,

THEM

stimulating himself as he buried his fingers-knuckle deep into her soft, velvety tunnel. She was tight, but he managed to cram in a fourth finger, causing her to emit a blood-curdling scream in response.

He reached for her internal nub and squeezed it hard between the nails of his thumb and index finger. She screamed so loud the blood vessels in her eyes could've ruptured at any moment.

"Oh yeah, squeal like the little bitch you are. Zoo-wee little piggy."

He didn't let up, he pinched tighter, imagining that he was popping an un-ripened grape. Her shrill yowls turned guttural and raspy. She thrashed her hips and knees around in an attempt to get him to release, but this inspired the inverse effect. He had instead begun to dig his dirty nails into her clit, drawing blood.

He released her.

He brought his hand to his crotch and rubbed his pulsating bulge. Jeanette looked down and saw a line of blood trickling down from the mound of her pubis. Her vagina burned like it had been skewered with a flaming spike. She then looked at Shannon, who had now gone completely catatonic.

Just then, a bell by the door chimed.

A third man had arrived.

THEM

"Took ya long enough, boy!"

"Well hot damn. Joey, did find us some things we could use on our new pets?"

"I damn sure did! Here, hand over that ginger bitch."

Joey sauntered past Shannon and grabbed Jeanette by the chin. He pushed a finger past her lips, shoving several pills into her mouth. The cold bitter tablets danced around Jeanette's throat as Joey smacked her on the cheek.

"Swallow em', bitch. I know dirty sluts like you love to swallow."

Jeanette resisted, she tried to spit them out, but Isaac held the switchblade at Shannon's bobbing throat. And so Jeanette swallowed. She gulped back the pills, forcing them down her throat and gagging. The dryness in her mouth did absolutely nothing to help. She hoped and prayed that these pills would just kill her.

"They should kick in any moment now."

And they did.

Jeanette's bowels lurched as a sharp pain prodded her rectum. Joey snaked his arms around her as his father yanked down her pants. He cut through her bleeding underwear with the switchblade and tore it off. Her stomach roiled as gastric compressions stabbed at her pelvis. As she sucked in her next breath, the pressure in

THEM

her rectum expanded as a log of hot excrement slid past her sphincter and onto the floor in a soggy splat.

"Why..." Jeanette rasped.

"You better shut the fuck up, cunt."

Joey then picked up a clump of shit with his bare hand and smeared it on Shannon's face. He stuck his fingers into her mouth, "suck my hand clean, bitch." And she did.

Joey soaked his hands in the shit once more and digitally molested Shannon as his other shit-stained hand squeezed and yanked at her exposed breasts.

Isaac wrestled Jeanette to the ground. He held her down as he smeared shit on his exposed cock. Before Jeanette could take another breath, the teen thrust his cock all the way into her, right down to the hilt. Jeanette cried heavily, biting her lower lip. The pressure mounted in her crotch as the man mercilessly slammed into her bleeding cunt. She screamed and writhed as her tailbone grated against the tiles from the force of his thrusts. Glass shards dug into her back as she was thrusted into.

"Please..." Shannon said, at last.

"You cunts ain't going nowhere."

Hearing his merciless declaration, Shannon began wailing. Jeanette's body shook like an electric fuse had

THEM

short-circuited. She had never felt so violated in her entire life. Her inner world, her most personal and private realm was contaminated with abject filth. She'd officially lost all control–her very humanity had been permanently damaged forever.

The man grabbed Jeanette's knife and held it to the side of her head.

"Hey fellas, look what I found."

"Oh yeah, what's a pretty bitch like you doing with something like that?"

"I bet this idiot thought she was gonna stick us with this."

"We oughta teach this slut a lesson, whaddaya say boys?!"

"Yeah, why don't we stick that knife all the way up her shit-caked ass!"

He threw his head back and laughed.

A gurgling sound was followed by the reek of urine. Jeanette looked to the side–both men had their cocks out and were urinating on Shannon's face and breasts. She tried to block them by pulling her legs up and curling into a fetal position on her side, but the blonde man kicked and stomped on her so hard that her body violently spasmed.

The father pinned Shannon's leg down as the other

THEM

took her gun and brough the butt-end down on her knee cap. Her head jerked out as she emitted an ungodly yelp as the bone caved in. He stomped on her knee until the popping sound of tendons and bone rattled the entire room. Shannon retched and threw up all over herself.

"Please... please don't hurt her anymore." Jeanette's pleas were met with a harsh slap to the right side of her face. The open-handed strike landed so hard her molars ground into one another. The taste of metal discharge leaked where she'd been hit.

The man passed Jeanette's butcher knife to Shannon's assailant. He grabbed a hold of Shannon's firm breast and buried the tip of the knife into her nipple. She cried and hollered as he dug his finger into the fatty fissure in her mutilated breast. He leaned down and bit the tip of her nipple, using his teeth to gnaw at the mauve bud. It was bloody and rubbery, and he chomped down on it and yanked his head back. He spat her nipple across the room and continued to work on her other breast. The other man straddled Shannon's head and slid his erect penis between the cleavage of her bleeding, mangled breasts. He slid into her fleshy canyon; leaking fat served as adequate lubricant.

THEM

"Yeah fuck those sweet, sweet titties, boy! Hurry up cuz I wanna eat the other 'un!"

"Almost there. Little man's about to explode!"

"Squirt on her big titties! Go on!"

"Oh fuck!" he grunted as pearlescent white beads jetted out of his cock slit and pinkened as they mixed with Shannon's blood.

"Damn, son. You've really been saving up all that ball snot now, haven't ya?"

"F-Fuck yeah."

They laughed as Shannon whimpered.

The red-haired man gave Jeanette's pebbled nipple a sloppy, wet kiss. Jeanette shut her eyes as he sucked on her hardening nipple. He clamped his lips around her nipple and chewed. A cold, searing jolt of electricity sparked on Jeanette's breast, causing her to yowl and buck upward from the hips.

A cold ridge of metal slid beneath the lobe of her ear. Before she knew it, the knife had been thrust into the cartilage, tearing the ear off with the merciless force of a wolf mangling its prey. Cold metal slid into her flesh like butter. It cut into the plastic tendon as meat separated from bone. The pain seared the entire left side of her face—blood leaked into her ear canal as the cords of muscle were jerked clean from her skull.

THEM

"This'll teach you to not be such a stuck-up bitch."

He shoved her knees apart and brought the dismembered ear to her crotch. He plunged it into her. He pulled the ear out and shoved it back in—in and out, violently pounding his knuckles into her pubic bone as he finger-fucked her bleeding pussy with her own ear.

Shannon looked oddly detached, her eyes were glazed-over as if she were in some kind of religious trance. Tears welled in her unblinking eyes as the men violated her. Her legs were roughly parted, causing her to involuntarily gasp. Though nothing could prepare her for the sharp, agonizing pain she felt as the steel butcher knife tore into her vagina.

Joey laughed like a maniac as he raped her cunt with the butcher knife, pulling it out only to shove it back in deeper. He slid it in and out, eviscerating her vaginal wall. Shannon's wails grew unrelenting. She tried to bring her knees together, but the other man kept her legs pried wide and open. She squirmed and screamed as Jeanette's butcher knife became an instrument of her brutal violation. His final thrust went in so deep the serrated edge of the knife jammed into her pubic bone. Her pubic area had been devastated beyond recognition.

He then cut a slit into her guts and dug into the

THEM

oozing cave. Out came pulpy bits of tangled clumps from her yawning cavern. This was accompanied by hot spurts of gas and jets of squirting blood. Crimson sludge belched out of Shannon as the beast dug into the veiny, intestinal tissue. Shannon's pink tendrils reminded Jeanette of earthworms crawling upon one another. Plasma and feces intermingled with sweat and decay.

"Yeah stick it in that bitch, daddy!"

The father straddled Shannon's midsection and submerged his cock into her entrails. He thrusted forward and back into her guts as he stiffened into his pulsating climax.

Jeanette could no longer scream; she was too taken aback by these abhorrent actions.

Joey then plunged his thumbs into Shannon's eye sockets. Orbital fluids oozed out beneath the beds of his grimy thumbs as her eyelids pooled with blood. The father sank his fingers deep into the recesses of her entrails. Shannon thrashed and shook involuntarily. They groped at her mutilated breasts and entrails like a pair of feral apes. They moaned and shuddered as if this defilement of an innocent woman's body had aroused their sexual instincts.

The torment still wasn't enough.

THEM

The bald man raked Jeanette's knife across Shannon's face, tearing through her flesh like it was made of soggy napkins. Her face had become a wet mask of rubbery skin. One man returned to the scene with a fire extinguisher and bashed her skull in until gray matter hiding behind her eyes spumed out of her splintered cranium in milky secretions. Shannon's screams ceased; all that could be heard was the gargling of thick blood.

"Her titties ain't as big, but I like them so much better."

"Ain't nothing compared to this blonde slut's massive knockers."

Heartache left Jeanette short of breath. Her entire chest had gone beet-red in response to the humiliation of being viciously violated by this stranger. Her face began to heat up in abject fury.

She was severely dehydrated; despite her best effort to cry, she could no longer wrench out a single tear. She tried to scream but found that she couldn't–her attacker's meaty hands were clamped around her throat. Her eyes swam in salty pools of red, her cheeks pinkened from the lack of oxygen.

"Yeah, fuck that little piggy up!"

"I can't wait to barbecue that slut's ass."

THEM

"Hey, we should spit-roast her and feed her to mom and Annie without telling them!"

"Cum in her shit-caked asshole and switch with me!"

"Yeah, let me take a nibble of them tasty tits!"

"Hey, I wanna fuck the live one now! This slab of meat is all cold and stiff."

The man released her neck, then punched her again and again right in the center of her face. He pummeled her breasts and neck, then hauled her up and slammed her face on his knee several times. He sucker punched her so hard in the gut her tender bladder burst; blood, urine, shit, and semen trickled down her gashed legs. Her face was so bruised and beaten it looked as if golf balls had been implanted beneath the layer of her skin. Thick clots of blood hung from her crooked nose.

"Move its leg, I wanna try fucking it sideways."

"Can you go look for a stick of butter? I wanna see if I can stick my fist up this fat bitch's ass!"

"Aww yeah stick yer pecker right in that bloody slit!"

"I bet this gal was raped by her daddy. I bet daddy threw her to his friends and forced her to suck cock all night long."

Jeanette's vision tripled. Waves of electric pain swam across her entire body. Her pain worsened when the men switched places—another one now raped her. He

THEM

turned her onto her side and fucked her sideways–his palm pressed the side of her head into the floor as he mounted her. He bucked into her even harder as his warm ejaculate filled her.

"Hey, if you open up her pussy like this it looks like a nice hairy clam! Say 'ahh' little pussy! Open wide!"

"I wonder if her cunt will taste like fish when we fry it."

"Aye, speaking of, does this place have a frozen foods section? I wanna stick a mackerel up the live one's pussy."

"I like the way ya think, boy!"

Next to her, Shannon's bones snapped and popped as her ribs separated. Skin, muscle, and bone parted with meaty tears. The man ripped open her chest cavity while the other went wrist-deep into her. When the second man withdrew his hands from her open chest, it looked like he had slipped on a pair of red gloves. He held a misshapen lump of muscle.

Shannon stopped thrashing.

"I guess nice girls die too."

All Jeanette could do was watch as they passed Shannon's heart around. They took turns biting into it. They chewed, spat, and bit into the thick muscle until it looked like nothing more than a pulverized slab of beef.

THEM

The older son then turned to Jeanette with a smile: "you're next, bitch."

"We're gonna fuck you dead. We just need to pack your little friend up into the truck."

The other two men grabbed Shannon's body by the arms and dragged her toward the door.

THEM
CHAPTER 9

Isaac leaned in close to Jeanette.

"Any last words, cunt?" he sneered.

Jeanette took this as her cue to act. She spat a glob of blood she'd been nursing directly into his eyes.

It sprayed out of her mouth, blinding him. The two collapsed onto the shelf behind them. Jeanette then grabbed the can of insecticide spray that landed next to her and sprayed it at his face.

"Owww fuck! Fuck you, bitch. I'm gonna kill you, you fucking bitch!"

Jeanette darted past him, but he pinned her against the refrigerators. She slid down under him, and flung the glass door open, shattering it on his face. She pulled glass bottles out and smashed them on his skull, one after the other.

"Fuck! You! I'll kill you; you rat bastard!" She shrieked.

She swung the broken glass at the man's face, tearing his temple open. The damage she'd inflicted was so severe a swath of bone emerged beneath the canyon of muscle. Gouts of blood raced down the left side of his face. She grabbed a fistful of his hair and yanked his head backward. She began to then repeatedly strike the

THEM

bridge of his nose with the bottom of a glass bottle.

"Fuck you! Die!!!"

The glass bottle shattered his face and ruptured his cornea. The sharpness sank into his eye, popping it like it was a poached egg. Goops of orbital sewage oozed out of his eye like uncooked yolk. Fragments of the bottle tore into his nose partially exposing his nasal cavity.

Still, Jeanette was relentless.

She didn't see what she was doing–all she saw was deep red.

What is the point in surviving if I'm not willing to fight for my life?

She twisted the broken glass into his neck, then let him drop down to his knees.

"You fuck, you disgusting fuck!"

She shoved him to the ground and unbuttoned his pants, yanking them down. His penis was nothing more than a pink wedge peeking out of a tuft of mangled pubic hair. She gripped the bottle and thrusted it forward, embedding it into the base of his groin. She bit down on her lip, yanked the broken glass free, and unleashed a flurry of stabs at his crotch. The shards cut through the layer of skin, gritting against the mound of his pelvis. She pulled it out, then stuck it back in, twisting with finality. Blood spurted out, littering the

THEM

white tiles with a spray of deep crimson. She dug the blade in deeper, screwing it as she plunged into the meaty grime. Small glass shards stuck out of his mangled penis. His scrotum had burst open, revealing his ruptured testicles. The bulbs latched on by slim, purple wires.

She looked back to see if the other two had begun to make their way back.

There was still no sign of them.

She pulled open Isaac's jacket and searched him. Nothing in his breast pocket, nothing in his jacket. She searched his pants. One pocket had his wallet. She rifled through the contents of the wallet but was unable to find what she was after.

She patted his other pocket—her breath caught in her throat as she felt that familiar outline. Refusing to let herself have any false hope, she slid her fingers into the man's pocket, and felt the cool, jagged metal. She gripped it, pulled it out, and held it up to her face.

The keys to their truck.

She hid behind one of the walls, looking at the convex mirror to see if she could spot them. There they were. Mere feet away from entering the convenience store. Her heart stopped mid-beat as thick acid bubbled up to her chest. The bell chimed, signaling their entrance.

THEM

"Alright, let's gut that other bitch now!"

"Hey, where's Isaac?"

Why did these mimics have names?

She couldn't afford to think anymore—all she could do was *do*. When they'd gotten far enough into the store, she sprinted.

"Hey! What the fuck!"

"Go get that bitch!"

Pushing past the door, she lunged forward into the daylight. Up ahead, she saw the SUV. She barreled forward, yanking the door open, and threw herself into the front seat. She jammed the key into the slot and twisted.

The car's engine revved to life.

The stench of Shannon's corpse in the car unnerved her.

When I figure things out, I am going to give her a proper burial.

She scanned her surroundings. The town was so desolate, yet in her mind's eye, beings lurked in the corner of every street. Her gaze flicked to the back—at the gas station; they were on her tail. Her head throbbed, matching the swift beat of her thudding heart. Her face melted with fatigue; her chest burned like it had been stung by a colony of fire ants.

THEM

"Come at me, you sick fucks!"

She floored the pedal like she was crushing a wasp nest. The tires screeched, rubbing out clouds of dirt as the car slammed directly into the men behind her. The impact was so tremendous Jeanette's entire body jumped. She didn't stop there, however: she pulled the clutch back and rolled over them, satiated by the hum of their skulls splintering against the wet road. White hot rage compressed to a boiling point in her chest. She wished she could revive them for the sole purpose of engulfing their faces with bullets until they looked like meaty sludge.

The dark thoughts invading her mind gave her pause.

Could I be on the verge of losing my humanity?

She thought about the pointlessness of it all—the fact that there was nothing she could possibly look forward to in a world like this.

Shall I just end it all now? Maybe I can save myself the heartache.

She thought about taking the broken bottle and burying it into the soft flesh of her wrist. She imagined drawing the blade down and unzipping her entire forearm, watching as the gooey mush of thick fluid pulsed out of the fresh tear.

She was then overcome by a latent feeling she'd had

THEM

deep within; a vigor boiling inside her brought forth by the survivalist instinct that had carried her through her entire life. The sudden wave of emotion stunned her, pushing her to plant her foot on the gas pedal and slap her hand on the steering wheel. She slapped herself in the face, forcing the much-needed adrenaline to kick in.

She'd long since given up thinking someone would save her.

She was all she had now.

THEM
CHAPTER 10

Jeanette put the truck in reverse, pulled on the stick, and swerved back onto the road. As she drove, the images she'd just seen replayed in her head. She knew there was no getting over this–there was no salvation for her. What had been done to Shannon, Samantha, and Alex would be burned in her mind for the rest of eternity.

She thought about how the men she'd just killed sounded normal. They walked like humans... there wasn't that uncanny awkwardness that *they* possessed. They didn't have that dead, glazed-over look in their eyes. Their eyes were wide with jubilation.

The more she replayed these events in her head, the more she pieced together the inconsistency. Could it be that, now that the rule book has been burned, humanity's actual instincts have finally been unleashed? Perhaps mankind truly was the worst thing to happen to this godforsaken planet; perhaps *we* were all just waiting for society to collapse so we could collectively lash out.

But how could we have turned into this so fast?

Jeanette floored the gas pedal and drove into the fog–speed limits no longer applied. She was going to see her

THEM

father.

As she entered the city, she could smell burnt rubber through the car's vents. The sight she bore witness to made her gag.

The entire city was up in flames.

The street was littered with human-shaped creatures reduced to their debased instincts. Human nature, in all of its destructiveness, was laid bare in all its brutal honesty. She stared at the road in front of her as her tongue became a leaden weight in her mouth.

"Oh my ... my ..."

Creatures tossed each other aside, tearing meaty lumps from each other's throats. One such beast took a bite out of a young boy's Adam's apple, revealing the off-white pipe of his esophagus. The road was strewn with corpses. Heads had been split open like cans of raw meat.

Jeanette would've assumed this was a nightmare, if not for the acrid stench of bile and tar. The entire city had been repurposed into an abattoir of viscera and debauchery. The pavement was rank with raw meat, bubbling blood, and feces.

Faces had been skinned, eyeballs had been gouged out, and excavated chest cavities lay open for the entire world to see.

THEM

A laughing woman plunged an ax into a man's head, bisecting his skull so quickly the cranial lobe divided into a meaty wedge. Blood sprayed out like an erupting volcano as the deceased man fell to his knees. All around Jeanette was a cacophonous din of screams of terror.

It was as if a rip in the universe had given her front row seats to the depths of hell itself.

Red ropes of intestines were torn from abdomens—weeping people were being raped with their own entrails. Children's heads were stomped on—cracked open like they were made of nothing more than shells containing congealed broth. All around her, anatomical parts littered the gravel like detritus after a storm. Jeanette sobbed so hard mucus ran down from her congested nose.

The fog had since subsided, yet not a single spot of sunshine glimmered through the thick clouds.

She turned onto the next curb and saw a man burying his teeth in another man's face. He was naked and on all-fours, bending over a corpse as he gnawed away at all the skin and fat, exposing the red musculature beneath. The corpse's flesh tore away from its skull in rubbery clumps as the beast bit into his yielding flesh. He smothered his sharp talon-like nails into the man's

THEM

abdomen, clutching at his innards with greedy, gore-stained hands. The man's entrails were rubbery, fluid-filled sacs that burst as the fiend bit into them. He looked up at Jeanette and smiled. His teeth were packed with fragments of meat.

Next to him, a demented woman with razor-sharp canines groped at a dead teen's breasts, like she was trying to burst a water balloon. She lowered her head and stuffed the premature breast into her mouth, sawing into it with her yellow gnashers. Clumps of frothy spittle spilled from her mouth as the cream-colored fat seeped out of the girl's ruptured breast. The teen's skull had been bashed in so horribly it looked like a deep red crater of jellied slime.

All around her, people were erupting in screams as if they were being slowly lowered into a fire pit. The repugnant sound inched its way into Jeanette's head and stewed into her muscles and sinew. The thought that these atrocities would be a part of her forever sent her stomach into a foul roil.

"No..."

She drove into the intersection where the source of the screams came from.

She wanted to turn around, but she was so close to her father's building—she wanted to look away, but

THEM

doing so would render her unable to navigate. By virtue of her mission, she was forced to take in the repugnant scene.

Unable to take it any longer she stopped the car, leaned forward, and vomited. The brown puke landed on her bare feet as she keeled over and coughed out a string of foamy saliva. She retched and gagged yet couldn't vomit anything more than vinegar water. She craned her head up, gripping the steering wheel as she sobbed.

She imagined her father sitting next to her telling her everything was going to be alright. She knew that if he was with her, he'd tell her to harden her hide if she wanted to survive. His love was tender and forgiving, yet tough when it counted.

She gazed up at the road again, starting the car.

A young girl who couldn't have been older than seven lay in front of the car, half her face had melted like the bubbling wax of a candle. Most of her skull had been burned, leaving only patches of dry hair on her sizzled scalp. Her eyeballs popped and bubbled from the intense heat–the glassy fluid leaked down her cheek like viscid egg whites.

An infantry of corpses littered the streets; their muscles turned black from the flames. Hues of white

THEM

bone and yellow fat were exposed around and beneath the charred muscles. Flesh began to redden and blister as it was exposed to fire.

As she drove further into the chaos, she saw flesh hanging in gummy chunks from dismembered limbs. Bodies hung from makeshift nooses; their arms and legs had been hacked off, leaving hollow caves where joints once were. Clumps of hanging entrails that resembled red vines blackened to a bubbling crisp as they were exposed to the fire.

A living woman was held down by her hands and feet—her eyes had been gouged out, leaving nothing but two black holes on her face. Her nipples were being burned with a lighter—smoke sizzled from her pustulating flesh as her body shook spasmodically. A trio of men masturbated at the loathsome sight of her as the two others cheered. Other corpses were so mangled and violated it was hard to tell where their torso even began.

"This isn't real. This isn't fucking real." Jeanette said to herself.

She pinched her eyes shut, willing everything to disappear, only to open them and take it all in once again.

A man who had been sawed in half lay naked on the

THEM

ground. His upper half was completely unrecognizable. An insane woman repeatedly bludgeoned with a crowbar. The woman laughed maniacally as she beat him to death and beyond. All that was left was a pulpy broth of brain matter encased in a mangled dish of bone. The woman looked back at Jeanette–she looked just like Anna.

No, this *was* Anna.

The man's bottom half was propped on its knees as a young boy sodomized him. The boy–who looked like he was in the second grade–bucked back and forth, pumping his underdeveloped penis into the corpse's anal cavity. His eyes, like the rest of *them,* had the vacant look of a meth addict. The corpse's guts lay dispersed as they slid back and forth in time with the kid's aggressive thrusts. The youth then pulled out his cock and replaced it with his entire fist. *He* dug his fingers into the man's anus as if he were digging for treasure. As he fist-raped the corpse, he stroked his half-hardened cock like he was attempting to tear it off. His tongue flicked in and out of his mouth as his eyes rolled to the back of his head. The little boy pumped his tiny prick so hard a string of blood spurted out of his purple urethra.

"W-why..." Jeanette whimpered, "I... I want to go

THEM

home..."

But where is home?

Was it back where she came from—where her dog lay dissected on the living room floor? Was it where her father was—an apartment with a malicious carbon copy of her? Was it the mere twenty-four hours earlier when the pitiful life she endured morphed into something she now dreaded? *I can't dwell on these thoughts anymore,* she thought, *I need to try and save dad so we can wait this madness out together.*

Where was the military? Where were the tanks? Was no one coming to help? Was it like this all over the country—no, the world? She had no way of checking. She drove across and over the anatomical parts that were once people and turned into the intersection that led to her father's building.

After about fifteen minutes of driving, she reached the end of the city, where the overpass was that led out of state. Her father's dilapidated building towered in front of her.

THEM
CHAPTER 11

The sun had not been seen all day. It was hidden behind a wispy patch of dark clouds. The overcast sky bleached the entire city with a monochrome shade. The streets were empty, yet Jeanette couldn't swallow the feeling of being watched.

She was a pessimist by nature, a glass-half-empty kind of person. She knew the situation was dire, but she still tried to find it in herself to recontextualize it in her head. She tried to battle against every lived experience that informed her worldview and gave herself the positive spin first: she was finally going to see the person who mattered most to her in her life. Yet the thought that the mimic could've hurt him still lingered in her mind, refusing to grant her even a slight semblance of peace. Still, she knew her father more than anyone else–he was a brave, discerning man who would eventually put two-and-two together. Should the mimic dare try anything on him, she trusted that he was strong enough to fight it off. Even at the age of fifty-nine, he exercised almost every day and was well-built.

"I'm coming, dad…" she whispered to herself.

Perspiration was glued to her face. Her dampened

THEM

clothes were plastered to her body. The glass door to the entrance was as shattered as her heart. She balled her hand into a fist and trudged forward into the decrepit lobby.

It was empty.

Naturally, neither elevator worked. She looked at the flight of stairs and gulped back a wad of spit. She wondered if she had the strength to make the upward hike. *What if some of them are in there, waiting for me?* She banished the thought as soon as it came.

"It's empty... it's empty... it's empty..."

She paused, took a deep breath, held it for ten seconds, then slowly blew it out of her mouth. Still, she was completely frozen; paralyzed from the waist down. She rubbed the palm of her hand on her chest and kneaded the patch of skin above her stammering heart.

"Alright, Jeanette... just one step. One little step..."

A shudder crawled up her spine. She shuffled her right foot forward, then her left. The immense pain of her anxiety vacuumed her lungs and clawed at her mind. A tingling sensation ran across her vertebrae with each footfall.

Her eyes were drawn to the doorway–the dark rectangular pit which could lead to either her last hope or her ultimate undoing. Her heart stammered as if it

THEM

were on the verge of exploding in her chest—it secreted molten lava in her lungs. Her skin was as pale as milk, and her bruised face had turned blue and purple. She feared that her father would now only have her voice to recognize her.

She walked up the flight of stairs, hand clenched on the old, rusted banister as she trudged upward.

Whoever designed the floorplan of the building crafted it in such a way that you'd have to walk across to the other side of the hall once you reached the top to make it to the next flight of stairs. Once she made it to that second row of steps, it would—hopefully—be smooth sailing from there.

Alright. Keep calm, Jeanette. Don't panic, you've already made it this far. You're already here.

It was supposed to be a simple task. Walk up the stairs. Walk across to the other side, take the next flight of stairs. It was supposed to be as easy as a walk in a breezy park, so why did she feel like someone was about to grab her from behind? She looked back, only to see an empty staircase. The stairs widened, the walls expanded and contracted, nausea crept in as her head tilted forward. She breathed in and gazed back up at the row of steps in front of her.

"One... two.... One... two..." She chanted to herself,

THEM

slowly exhaling.

In spite of her father's cruel words, she still tried to hold on to the hope that he was still alive. She mined this thought until she found that small nugget of golden hope she'd yearned for. That longing—despite very well being a pipe dream—was something she held on to. It was like carrying a small piece of home with her no matter how difficult life had become.

Still, her paranoia froze her. She embraced herself, shivering like she was on a snowy mountain with nothing more than a quilt to warm her.

Jeanette made a feeble attempt at quickening her steps, yet doing so kindled a fire in her pelvic floor. She touched the wetness in her crotch and inspected her hand: her fingers were wet with blood. She'd definitely incurred vaginal tearing from the brutal assault. Her aching groin felt like someone had reached their claw into her lower torso and squeezed her organs from the inside. The soreness sent shockwaves of electricity to the center of her hip flexors and down the base of her spine.

Jeanette shook her head in an effort to clear space for rational thought. Forcing her dry eyes to open wider, she pushed past the tender pain of exhaustion throbbing between her eyebrows. Her eyes felt heavier

THEM

than anvils as she fought to stay conscious. Her entire world spun on its axis. She leaned on the wall, desperate to lie down and get some much-needed sleep.

With each step forward the area between her hips and pubic bone screamed out for relief; she wished she could sit on some ice to numb the pain. The movements she made were so forceful her chest felt like it was about to implode, making her release an outpour of dry coughs.

Atop the stairs, the shadowy hallway in front of her stretched on for miles. It was dark and still. There wasn't any movement, yet she couldn't ignore the queasiness in her stomach that came with last night's emergency alert system.

An eerie silence blanketed everything.

She didn't want to take another step–doing so would alert whomever...whatever was awaiting her.

Just then, the click of a door rattled her. The corner of her eye caught something blurry–some subtle motion of a tall figure shaking like the tail of a rattlesnake. She faced it head on, gripping the edge of the door as she prepared to slam it shut. It hunched over, sauntering around with a lilting gait. She couldn't tell if it had noticed her. She looked around to find something to

THEM

defend herself. Luckily, the old building had been under construction recently, so a pile of bricks sat in the far corner. She picked one up, steadying herself for the incoming threat.

She knew what these things were capable of doing– she knew there was no way in hell she could appeal to their compassion. She was a frightened child hiding from the monster in her closet. Except the monster in her closet had now been unleashed on the entire world: and *they* looked like people.

Some of them actually were.

Something pounded on the door behind her.

"Help, help me for fuck's sake help! Anyone!" A man cried out in the darkness.

He pounded on the door so hard it violently kicked against Jeanette's back. Many people lived on this floor, yet no one answered him. No one wanted to help. Was this what humanity had become? Was this what it always was? Were there truly no good Samaritans? Guilt crawled around in Jeanette's gut, worming its way up to her tightened chest.

Perhaps, deep down, I am like them.

Perhaps, no matter how civilized or educated we are–in the end, we are all just wolves disguised as men. Perhaps they are just the most honest version of

THEM

us. Perhaps the biggest mistake was, indeed, mercy. In a world such as this—one that sees not in shades of grey, but red—mercy is nothing more than stupidity.

In the end, no one is truly innocent.

Jeanette was flattened by her despair.

She stood up and turned toward the narrow, rectangular glass. The man's gaze locked on hers. Fear paralyzed her. His sunken eyes widened, and all the blood drained from his pale, fear-contorted face.

"I knew it! I knew there was someone there. Hurry up and unlock the fucking door—please!"

Should I open the door? If I do, his attacker might come in and kill us both! But I can't just let him die! I can't—

Her train of thought was interrupted by his screaming pleas, "Please, help! He's coming! Hurry up you dumb fucking bitch he's going to fucking kill me, hurry up!!!"

"I—" her voice cracked.

She reached for the lock, then drew her hand back as if she'd just touched the scalding metal of a tea kettle. Her thoughts pinballed in her head. Her frenzy was heightened by his hyper shrieks.

"Hurry the fuck up, you dumb cunt!!"

Hurry up and open the door, Jeanette. Just do it. Stop over-thinking. He's going to fucking die! Do it

THEM

now!!! Hurry!!! Time is running out if you don't he will–

Three dark shapes sped across the hallway behind him. They moved so erratically it reminded Jeanette of looking at something through an unfocused camera lens. In a last-ditch effort at survival, he started banging his skull on the plexiglass. He slammed his head into it so hard a fissure split open. Blood gushed down his forehead and splatted onto the glass like squashed tomatoes. He clawed at the glass, letting out another wave of blood curdling screams.

What was she going to do? Risk her own life for that of a stranger? She knew she could have saved him–but if the events of this morning and last night and this morning showed her anything, risks of that sort were out of the question. And on the off chance that she did save him, she didn't want to get emotionally attached to someone she knew she was going to inevitably lose.

"I'm sorry..." she whispered.

Jeanette turned her back to him.

She couldn't take it anymore–this, all of this–what even was the point? Her own death was something she'd never thought of because of how she had a habit of going out of her way to find distractions to not have to contemplate her mortality. Now, everything was

THEM

different—her death felt like an inevitability. It was only a matter of time.

Hating herself, she leaned on the banging door and slumped down to the floor.

The banging stopped.

His yells turned into gurgles. Something wet sprayed on the glass. The sound of fabric being torn was met with a distinct snap and crunch she'd come to know all too well. The man's gurgling screech stopped, bringing forth a chorus of shrill cackles that reminded her of the chirping noise bats make to welcome the night. It went on for ages.

"Stop. Stop. Stop. Stop. Please stop...." She begged.

She pressed the palm of her hands against her ears in a strained, albeit fruitless effort to muffle the sound.

The knocking began again.

This time it was less frantic—it was light and relaxed. *Could he have successfully fought the monster off?* She thought. She didn't see him carrying anything to defend himself, so it was highly unlikely. She remembered hearing something about people suddenly possessing superhuman strength in moments of extremely dire straits.

"Fuck it." She said.

She stood up to unlock the door but was stopped

THEM

when her eyes met the gaze in front of her. His slackened face stared back at her, but it was no longer attached to his body. It was held up by a hand, the hand was attached to a human-shaped fiend whose face was distorted in a massive, self-satisfied grin. His jagged, misshapen teeth clenched around the man's entrails. They hung like bruised snakes and bobbed up and down as the mimic chewed into them. He grinded his teeth left and right, sawing into the elastic membrane as fecal matter oozed out of its tears.

She recognized the monster's face.

A faint sliver of light illuminated his torso. He wore the uniform of a concierge. The same concierge who greeted her whenever she visited her father.

"Boris... no..."

He didn't move an inch. It was as if every single drop of blood had frozen in his veins. His skin was pale. Everything about him was *wrong*. Minutes passed and there was still no reaction, until he finally made a faint chuckling noise. It was as if he was laughing at her—at the fact that she had been such a coward in this man's time of need.

His head ticked to the side with a shrill, clicking noise. The features in Boris' face shifted. His flesh looked so pale it was almost translucent. He looked at

THEM

Jeanette with a lidless grin that stretched from ear to ear. His pupils appeared to vibrate.

His smile had grown so extensive—so exaggeratedly pulled back—it widened past the sides of his face. His teeth were black, and his fleshy gums grew more exposed as that wretched smile expanded. It ran past his ears and to the back of his head. Dead in the eyes, his pink tongue darted in and out of his mouth with lewd slurps.

"Taste, tasty cunt. Slurp and suck, suck, suck your tasty cunt. Bite into your clit and tear it out of your smelly pussy slit. Bleeding cunt yum-yum," he rasped.

Jeanette had been reduced to a scared kid. A hopeless child in desperate need of a lifeline. She was reminded of childhood—when she was home alone, and her parents weren't there to assure her there were no monsters in her closet.

"No..." is all Jeanette could say.

It banged the decapitated head on the glass one more time, producing the same knocking sound. It was a gruesome combination of meat, sludge, and bone. If Jeanette weren't so spent and dehydrated, tears would've likely rolled out of her sore eyes. She regretted everything.

I could've done something. I could've saved him. Why

THEM

didn't I? Why?!

Wetness percolated between her toes and by the soles of her feet. The stranger's blood seeped out from under the door. The growing puddle had completely drenched her feet; this scarlet, warm pool belonged to a living man just a few minutes ago–a man she failed to save. *But could I have saved him? Was he already a lost cause?* A bubble of regret built in her chest–if she moved an inch her entire torso felt like it would burst.

"Fuck you. Fuck you! Go to hell!!!"

She slammed her palms on the door and screamed. She didn't scream with fear–she'd long since gone past the point of fear. She screamed with fury; out of burning rage that clawed at every muscle and fiber in her body. She screamed at herself, wishing she'd had the courage to open the door for that innocent man. She screamed at *them,* cursing them for all they'd done. She screamed at all of the people who took this as an opportunity to indulge in their own sick desires, snuffing out all the happiness and innocence in the world because they knew no one would stop them. She screamed at the monster in front of her–the senseless killer who didn't have a single shred of life in his eyes, nor any semblance of human warmth. She imagined filling his skull with the bullets of Shannon's gun. She

THEM

screamed and cursed the damned day she was born. She spat at the glass, wishing her pink snot would have landed on the fucker's face.

Then she held back a sharp exhale–a breath that turned into a giggle, a giggle that mutated into uncontrollable laughter. *This is all just a nightmare, right? None of this is actually happening, right? I'm going to wake up any moment now, right? Right?!*

She laughed.

And laughed.

And laughed.

She threw her head back, gripped her ribs and scream-laughed hysterically.

It was a shrill guffaw akin to a hyena's cackle.

Something teetered in the distance. Shadows grew twenty feet tall from the bottom of the staircase.

Footsteps.

Breathing.

Her heartbeat stammered in her aching head.

She sank to the floor, huddling in a ball. She tucked her head between her knees and wrapped her arms around her shins. The footsteps became louder, and the presence of someone towering over her sent a faint pulse of electricity to the base of her spine.

THEM

"Miss?"

She stayed silent.

"Miss, are you alright? Do you need any help?"

No response.

"My name is Carter. Do you need help standing up?"

She ground her teeth so hard her entire head spasmed. Had she clenched any harder, her molars would have cracked. A shiver of pure revulsion burned in Jeanette's core.

"Yeah, I found someone by the door leading to the second floor–she seems to be hurt, she's not responding and there's blood all over the floor... no, I can't just leave her like this, can I? Be reasonable. Look, I—"

Jeanette lunged at the man. He fell back, and she straddled him. Blinded by rage, she screamed like a madwoman.

"Wait–miss, I just want to..."

The hatred bubbled up inside her until it reached a boiling point. Jeanette swung the brick down, striking Carter's cheek. It split his skin open. He tried to fight her off, but she struck him again–this time on his brow bone. The blow was so hard, the back of his head smacked against the concrete with a thick crack. The sorrow in his eyes meant nothing to her. His

THEM

benevolence, she believed, was just an act. He could be kind now, but it was only a matter of time before his ultraviolet urges materialized.

Bringing the brick down once more, she exposed the inner musculature of Carter's forehead–red muscles lay beneath a flap of rubbery flesh. She threw down another blow–it met him square on the bridge of his nose. The cartilage crackled as a burst of blood squirted on Jeanette's face. She raised the brick and brought it down on his other cheek, breaking through the skin and popping his hemorrhaging eye half-out of its socket. Moisture built beneath her crotch. He'd lost control of his bladder.

Carter's breaths were short and intermittent–a gargling came from his labored respirations. Jeanette struck him on the chin, then the mouth. His teeth chipped, and several popped loose. His lip ruptured and tore a line which led to the stump of his cracked nose. Jeanette hit him in the center of the face again as his skull caved inward. His nasal septum had disintegrated, leaving a pit where it had once been. Blood gushed out of the stump like a miniature tsunami. Still, she beat him–one successive blow after another.

She dug the edge of the brick into his eye; it deflated

THEM

like a crushed fruit. Blood ebbed out of his toothless mouth as he coughed. She grinded the gore-stained brick into his face, digging into it like she was grating a block of cheese. She brought it up again, after digging away the skin, and rained down another set of furious blows. She screamed as blood sprayed at her like water from a geyser. Chips of bone pierced through the tattered flesh as she beat him far beyond the threshold of expiration.

His body twitched a few times, before stilling completely.

What Jeanette stared down at wasn't a face—it was a cave. A cave with jagged edges and chunky liquid viscus. His tongue hung out of his dismembered jaw like a newly defrosted cold cut. His nasal cavity and eye sockets were crushed, rendering him unrecognizable.

Jeanette then sunk her fingers into the man's hairline, pulling his scalp back until the hair atop his head folded over the top of his spine. His head looked like it had exploded from within. The ground around them was bestrewn with ocular juice and brain matter. The milky flesh of his neck had been so drained of blood it looked like paper.

She stood up, looked at the not-Boris, and pointed the brick at him.

THEM

"You're next. Bitch." She growled through blood-stained teeth.

She gripped the doorknob and turned it. She flung the door forward and charged shoulder-first into the monster. It fell backward. She whacked it in the face three times with the brick, each blow landing with a wet, satisfying thud.

"Fuck you, mother fucker!!!"

With the speed of lightning, it grabbed her wrist, bending it so far the brick fell to the ground. A white-hot pain erupted at the join; her wrist snapped as he folded her palm onto the forearm. Before she could fight back, his fist sank so far into her gut, knocking the wind clean out of her. Liquid copper flooded her mouth. Blood and thick saliva spilled past her bottom lip with each subsequent breath. Boris' mimic tackled her to the ground, pinning her arms down over her head with one hand.

His putrid drool fell on her face in gelatinous strands. He bent down and licked her face. He tore open her blouse. Wind beat against her bare chest. He slid his fingers into her sweatpants and into her underwear.

"Tasty, tasty cunt."

She didn't relent. She craned her head upward and snapped at him. Her teeth caught his lower eyelid. He

THEM

shrieked as she yanked her head back, tearing a triangular patch of skin off his face. The tear exposed the lower portion of his eyeball, the layer of muscle over his cheekbone oozed gouts of blood. She thrashed and thrusted and cursed. She spat on his face and slammed her forehead into his nose.

As she maneuvered to bite him once more, he punched her in the gut again. She had nothing left to throw up, so the bitter taste of bile skidded to the back of her throat. He pinned her back down to the floor so hard the back of her head rapped against the tiles. He wrapped his hand around her neck, causing black dots to form in her vision. She tried to breathe in, but the air wouldn't move past her uvula.

"You die now, b—"

A blast of thunder lit up the entire room. Her vision came back into focus—the Boris mimic stilled. She then noticed the barrel of the gun pointed directly at the side of his head.

"Jeanette? Jeanette?! I'm so sorry I didn't believe you, my love. I'm so sorry..."

She couldn't accept that this was real. As far as she was concerned, she had been killed and was having that one final DMT hallucination.

"Come, let's go."

THEM

He nudged one hand under the small of her back, then the other on her upper back. He hoisted her up like he did when she was a young girl. This strong, beautiful man. The first man she ever loved. The man she admired every day of her life. Her king. She rested her head on his chest and closed her eyes.

Despite being unable to produce tears, she wailed and sobbed.

"Hush now, it's all going to be alright."

THEM
CHAPTER 12

Jeanette's muffled sobs were a survival song. She let it all out. All her emotions splayed out on the table for the man who saw her at her lowest lows and highest highs–the man who helped her through all of it. Once again, just like when she was a little girl, her father had saved her.

"How did you find me?" she croaked.

"Don't worry about that, Jeanette. You need rest."

In the apartment, Janice awaited them with a hot bowl of chicken broth and a side of buttered toast. It made Jeanette's stomach grumble; the warm meal practically called out to her, begging to be eaten.

Jeanette opted to have a shower first to address potential infection. As she stood under the warm water, her aching muscles soothed at last; it was like finally getting to collapse to the floor after running a marathon. She then slipped into a soft cotton bath robe. The warmth provided by the terry cloth and the cleanness of her skin was euphoric.

"Are you all done in there, dear?"

"Yes, daddy."

She hugged him once again. Her father tucked her into the guest bed and laid the tray over her lap. Janice

THEM

slowly spooned the onion soup into her mouth, blowing each spoon before she poured it in. When Jeanette finished, she lay flat against the pillow.

"Dad, what happened?"

"We don't know. There's no TV and no internet. The phone lines just stopped working too. I'm glad you managed to call me, otherwise I would've been killed by that *thing*."

"I'm glad too..."

"I'm so sorry, I should've known..."

"What happened to it?"

Her dad paused, regarding her silently. Then, "I interrogated her about your life. She wasn't able to answer any of the questions properly, so I snuck up behind her with my Beretta and killed her."

Relief descended on Jeanette's chest listening to this.

"Dad, I want to see it."

"I don't think that's a good idea."

Her senses kicked in; the relaxed state she was in had gone just as soon as it had come. The temperature in the room plummeted, and she began to smell something foul behind the door. A surge of unwelcome fear seized her heart.

She recalled that platitude he brought up whenever she was frightened.

THEM

"What do we say when we're scared, dad?" She said, grinning.

He didn't answer. He instead regarded her inquisitively, a yawning pause stagnated in the air of the room. Usually, he'd answer with a snap and offer her a cheeky wink. Heck, it was him who had come up with this phrase to begin with. So why wasn't he answering? Was this a joke? Was he pretending to not know?

"Dad. What do we say when we're scared?" she said again, this time with a cutting sternness.

The features in his face tightened.

"It appears that I've forgotten. Would you mind refreshing me?"

He scratched his head.

Her blood chilled.

An onslaught of pins and needles invaded the membrane coating her muscles.

"Show me the fucking body."

Her father looked at Janice.

She nodded.

"It's in the master bedroom."

Jeanette stared at the door for a while, then started toward it. She pushed past the two of them, ambled past the dining table, and gripped the doorknob leading

THEM

to the master bedroom. As she stood in front of the bedroom door, the presence of her father and Janice loomed behind her. She turned the knob and heard the sudden *click*.

She pushed the door open.

In front of her lay the outline of a body. She couldn't make out its features in the dark. Her heartbeat fluttered like the wings of a hummingbird as she felt around the wall for the light switch. Her skin crawled as it finally met the cold plastic.

She pressed down.

Click.

Lying in front of her wasn't a body. It was two bodies—neither of which belonged to her mimic.

The eviscerated corpses belonged to her father and Janice.

The inexplicable drop in temperature had plummeted even further—it was as if she'd just swam through a cold pocket in an otherwise sun-warmed lake.

She turned to them.

"What's wrong," Janice said, her smile as wide as the Cheshire cat's.

"I–I..." she stuttered.

Her words froze in her mouth.

Jeanette wasn't capable of screaming. Instead, she

THEM

watched in abject awe at the state she'd found herself in. Her father's mouth hung open; his eyes rolled back in his head turning into blackened orbs. Black, tar-like fluid secreted from his lips as he shook and clicked in front of her.

"Come to daddy."

She shoved past them, screaming, and flung open the front door.

In the apartment across from her, a woman stared in shock and disbelief. The woman, whose name was Angela Dawkins, extended her hand to Jeanette. She was clearly far more charitable and courageous than Jeanette had ever been. Before Jeanette could make it past the threshold and take Angela's hand, a firm arm locked around her neck.

"No! No! No! Please, I don't want to die!"

"Shh, baby. Daddy's got you..." he hissed into her ear.

She dug her nails into the doorframe, gripping it for dear life. It was of no use. Her nails peeled clean off the beds of her fingers as they scraped into the painted wood.

"No-o-o-!!! Please, no!!!"

The door slammed shut.

THEM
EPILOGUE

All Angela could do was listen in horror at the infernal cacophony in the apartment across hers. Feeling dejected and useless, she gently shut her door and sunk to the ground. Tears welled in her eyes as the screams from next door rang in her ears.

"Annie, I told you to not open that door."

"Sorry mom, I thought I'd go check on Isaac and Joey. They said they'd be back with the food hours ago!"

"Those damn boys. They can never get anything done on time. They really do take after your father."

"True."

"If they're not back in time I can just boil some pasta. There's enough for all of us."

"I don't know... pasta? It's Isaac's birthday. I wish we had the supplies to bake a cake for him."

"I know, dear."

"How long do you think it'll be before things are safe again?"

Angela's mother pulled her into a tight hug. Angela nestled her head into her mother's chest and shut her eyes. She tightened her embrace, seeking her mother's warmth and comfort. It was all she could do to calm herself after seeing the dread-filled look in that

THEM

stranger's eyes.

"I love you, mom."

"I love you too, sweet Annie."

The screams eventually died down.

After a long bout of silence, a faint cackle echoed through the walls.

The End

THEM

THEM

THE MIRROR GAME

A bonus short story

It's the fourth of July. The din of fireworks crackled outside my window, sending shockwaves of sound through the walls of my bedroom. The green and red lights glowed and bounced off my darkened walls.

I place the pillow over my head to muffle the sounds. It's not every day that it's this noisy—but it is every day that I find it difficult to fall asleep. Oddly enough, the fireworks relax me. They ease away the tension that accompanies the silences.

I can't remember the last time I managed to stay asleep for longer than two hours. I drift into the abyss, only to wake up in a cold sweat. Every night, I dream the same dream. I see a fiendish figure. It lurks in my mind. Is it all just in my head? Is he actually here? It's been like this since I was a naive child, and I've carried this abominable weight with me into my thirty-second year.

I'm now a third-grade social studies teacher—something I didn't predict I'd become since I didn't have many memories in school at that age. I figured this would hinder me from being able to connect with

THEM

the kids, but this setback didn't stop me from getting the job. I suppose life is just funny that way.

I didn't have many friends growing up. I recall purchasing a foil packet of trading cards just to have *something* that all the other kids did. I didn't care for the cards, per se... but without them, I wouldn't be invited to sit in a circle with my classmates at recess. It had eventually gotten to the point where I gave up on trying to understand the mechanics of these trading cards. I was flustered by the ever-changing rules of the game and all the character names. My cards wound up the trash at the end of the day.

I'd sit alone on the slides, munching on a granola bar, thinking of what it felt like to be one of them. One of the carefree kids who took their friendships for granted because they knew there'd always be someone waiting for them with an enthusiastic grin when the school bell rang.

I gave up on making real friends. So, I decided to supplement them with one of my own making. His name was Dylan. He'd sit next to me now, not saying anything. I did all the talking. He'd just be happy to listen–smiling and nodding along. I'd tell him about all the things I wanted to tell the other kids–about the shows I watched, or the sports I couldn't stand. And so

THEM

Dylan and I existed in our own bubble away from all the hubbub. He and I were perfectly content with having school pass us by, rather than having it be the worst experience in our lives.

The Fourth of July fell on a Friday. My parents asked me if I had a sleepover planned. The answer was always 'no'. As a result, they hired a babysitter to look after me since they were planning on staying out late. I told them I wanted to come with them because I'd never been to a party. They insisted that this party was *adults only*. At my age now, I know what this means—back then, I'd felt utterly dejected. Wasn't one's family supposed to have one's back? Didn't they see how lonely and despondent their own child was? Couldn't they just stay *here* for a few hours and play board games with me until I fell asleep?

"No, you can do that when Nadia gets here. She's not a lame babysitter. It'll be fun!"

"Lighten up, son. I'll take you out to ice cream on Sunday, and you can have whatever you want."

That's all that was said. They each planted a kiss on my head before heading out. Nadia arrived about a half-hour later. She had raven hair with red streaks, her nails were painted a shade of glistening onyx, and her arms were adorned with punk rock tattoos.

THEM

I bet my parents would freak out if I ever dressed like that when I became a teenager.

She sat on the couch, watching HBO. I wasn't allowed to watch anything other than Cartoon Network and Disney.

"Hey, Jeremy, sit next to me."

"I'm not allowed to watch that channel."

"Why not?"

"It's for grownups. If mommy and daddy find out, I'll get grounded."

"They're not going to find out, dude."

"H-how?"

"I won't tell if you won't," she said, offering me a wink.

And so I sat next to her, riveted by what was on the screen. A girl named Sally was chased around by a masked man with a loud weapon... one that I'd eventually come to learn was a chainsaw. I couldn't take my eyes off the screen, even though the entire final act of the film gave me a headache from all the screaming.

"I bet your friends aren't as brave as you, kid. When I was your age, I would've been scared shitless if I tried to watch this."

Despite my curiosity, I didn't want to admit to her

THEM

that I was, in fact, terrified. I told her I didn't have any friends. She didn't believe me. Everyone my age had friends—it was at this age when making friends was the easiest. No hormones or drama, is what she said. I had no idea what she was talking about. Eventually, I conceded and told her that I had a friend and that his name was Dylan.

"Oooh, where does he live?"

"He lives here."

Her complexion blanched at the mention of it. I instantly regretted telling this person—who I hadn't even known an hour prior—one of my biggest secrets. I couldn't trust her, yet here she was prying me on things only to leave me feeling judged.

Just then, her silent gasp of an expression morphed into something more quizzical.

"Oh, so like, an imaginary friend?"

"I hate to admit it, but yeah."

"Cool."

"What?" I said, utterly bemused by her outright nonchalance.

"You know, there's no such thing as an imaginary friend. You're just special. I'm special too."

Something warm in my chest blossomed at her compliment. I'd never been good at taking

THEM

compliments, but I enjoyed them, nonetheless. I had no friends, and I didn't have the highest grades—all I'd ever known was scorn and criticism. I didn't wake up this morning thinking I'd feel this cheerful, but I embraced it.

I'd told my parents about Dylan. My father didn't approve. My mother encouraged it because she said it was good for my creativity, and that most other kids had one as well. As far as I knew, they didn't—but she certainly wasn't going to hear that from me. She said it was merely a coping mechanism I had adopted after moving from New York to this small town in Idaho for my father's business. She didn't blame it on my social anxiety because that was something she'd always denied I had.

According to Nadia, imaginary friends were people who existed in other dimensions. The only reason I could see them was because I had this thing she called a *third eye*. Apparently, this unique gift enabled me to communicate with beings from beyond the fold and find friends that were far better than anything I could have in this world. She said she could help strengthen my abilities by playing a game.

It was called *The Mirror Game*.

And who was I to deny her? She was the first person

THEM

to make me feel this hopeful after a long time. She was the only one who's listened to me instead of casting me aside.

The Mirror game had a strange set of rules. She dictated them to me, but she also wrote them down on a piece of scratch paper just in case. The objective was to open myself up to the possibility of welcoming Dylan into this world. It had to be done in the bathroom, while I was all alone. She'd taught me how to light a match, and we'd practiced several times in order to get it right. She'd handed me a red candle from the dining table and sent me to the powder room.

"Listen to me carefully, Jeremy. The rules of the game are simple."

I nodded, swallowing back a gulp.

She took both my hands in hers.

"First, you have to be alone. Second, you need to drench this washcloth with rosewater and rub a circle on the mirror thirty-three times in order to activate the portal. Count out loud so you don't lose track. Third, light the candle and set it down in front of yourself. Fourth, turn off the lights. Fifth, read what I've written down on the paper, and look at the center of your forehead in the mirror after saying each line. The words on the page aren't in English, but I wrote them down

THEM

phonetically so you can pronounce them correctly. Sixth, stare at that same point in your forehead until the rest of your face is blurred. Don't stop thinking of Dylan. Lastly, trust what you see and don't look away until Dylan says your name. Any questions?"

"Y-yeah... I don't know how to pronounce this word."

"Here, let's go through it again. Let me hear you say the chant once more time."

The skin on my face prickled with feverish calcification. A thick batter of watery filth caked my consciousness, causing a series of shudders to race through me. Frightened, I took shallow breaths as my heart beat hastened like the wings of a mosquito. By then, my face had become so blurry that it was unrecognizable—my eyes were down to my chin, my jaw had been elevated past my nose, my nose to my forehead... It was all so wrong. I closed my eyes.

"Jeremy" a gravelly voice hissed in my ear.

I snapped my eyes open. The mirror had transformed into a running sheet of black ink. The dense temperature in the room had dropped. It felt as if I had been wading through freezing molasses. As I exhaled, a plume of vapor billowed out of my mouth. The fire on the candle burst past my vision, spearing upward about five feet high to the ceiling. I shuffled two steps back,

THEM

until someone pressed a hand to my shoulder. I yelped and spun around. Just as I was about to see who it was, the candle was snuffed.

I was all alone in the bathroom.

"N-Nadia?" I mewled.

No one answered. I seized the doorknob and twisted it, only for it to get stuck half way through my rotation. I cranked it again, yielding the same ghastly result. Again and again I forced and pulled. Tears stung my eyes as I yelped and screamed, banging on the door.

"Nadia let me out! Nadia!"

I was met with indifferent, deafening silence. Minutes passed, and the effect was disorienting. I couldn't see my hand in front of my own face. Even the light that trickled in under the door slat from the living room had been switched off. My skin prickled, and my senses heightened as if alarming me that something else was in the room.

"Jeremy..."

That same guttural voice. It sounded like it came from the depths of a drain pipe, yet the person speaking was inches away from my face. My body felt like it was being pulled toward it. I figured that if this really was Dylan, perhaps touching him would somewhat ease my trepidation. As I reached out, an agonizing shockwave

THEM

erupted in my core. My eyes screamed in pain—the sensation was that of being blinded by needles. My chest caved into the tormenting soreness as the pressure in my ribs dug into me like talons. The throbbing burn spread its way from my chest to my pounding head. It felt like my skull was splitting open and my ear drums were being tortured by a frequency that would shatter the sound barrier!

My next memory was waking up in a hospital bed. A cannula was wedged into my nose, aiding my respiration. The drowsiness had abated. It was as if I'd awoken after a long night's sleep. My mother's tear-stained face concerned me. My father stood stoically beside her. Both wore what they'd had on when they left for the party. Outside the window it was daylight. Had I really been out cold this entire time?

My parents took turns chiding me, but it was nearly impossible for me to absorb what they said as I was in this state.

"Nadia called us saying you had a seizure. What on earth were you doing in that bathroom, son?"

"No, she said you went in there on your own. Are you calling her a liar?"

"Jeremy, listen... Dylan is not real. There's no portal to whatever it is you're saying in our bathroom mirror.

THEM

This will be the last I hear of it, please."

Except, the seizures and panic attacks never ceased. I was met with an army of therapists who came and went. Every time I attempted to recall the events of that fateful night to them, all I could see was a sinkhole of tar as deep as a demon's maw. The night terror became more frequent. The first time I communed with Dylan, after the events in the bathroom, was after I'd been assaulted by an especially rough nightmare. I woke up with a start, scanning my room for fragments from my dream. Once my eyes adjusted to the darkness... I detected the shape of a man in the shadowed corner.

"Dylan?"

"Dylan, is that you?"

"Dylan, please answer me..." I sobbed.

My mother tried to settle me down every time the nightmares–which I couldn't recall the second I woke up–plagued me. Father was far less patient. There was absolutely no way either of them would believe me.

"Are you seriously asking me if there's a fucking ghost in your room?"

"Stuart, language!"

"No, Diane. I've had enough of this. It's ridiculous already–this kid is too old to be spewing this kind of nonsense."

THEM

"Look Jeremy. I'll only say this once: it's all in your head."

"Fine! I'll let the dog sleep in his room. Just this once. I better not hear any more of this ghost crap afterward."

They'd heard enough about ghosts and Dylan, so I tweaked my story. I told them there was a man in my room. It was a lie, but only partially so. I knew what I saw whether or not either of them would believe me. There had been a series of break-ins in the area, and they were nervous that a pedophile had maybe found his way into the upstairs room.

They'd called the police the following day, yet nothing pointed to forced entry.

I slept in a sleeping bag on the floor of their room for a few nights, until they added more locks to my window. I begged them to let me stay with them for one more night, but I was banished back to my own room.

By nine in the evening, I found myself sleepy and ready to turn in for the night.

"Goodnight," mother said, guiding me under the warmth of my duvet. She shut the door behind her. I then shut off the lamp, crawled under the covers, and drifted into nothingness.

THEM

I was awoken by something wet. The tender brush of Sammy, our Labrador, licking my hand. Sammy usually slept in my parents' room, but mom probably agreed to let him keep me company tonight. I patted the bed, inviting him to hop in with me. Moments passed, yet I never felt him climbing onto the bed. I assumed that he had probably gotten confused and gone to sleep on the floor.

I switched on the lamp, squinting as I calibrated all the light that had just infiltrated my gaze. As I rubbed my eyes, the blurriness that fogged my vision gradually took in the rest of the room. Sammy wasn't lying next to me, nor was he at the foot of my bed. I checked under the bed to see if he'd be there, but he wasn't. I scanned the rest of the room again, but it was completely empty.

"Sammy?"

I was met with no response other than resounding silence.

"S-Sammy?" I tried again, as the shivers took hold of me. There was no response.

Hopelessness flattened me. I switched the light off, only to see that same figure of a man in the corner. Panicking, I switched the night lamp back on. I made an effort to sleep, but after every ten seconds or so, my

THEM

eyes opened to survey the room. I willed my aching eyes to stay shut so I could drift back into what I hoped would be a restful slumber. All my efforts, however, were for naught; my alert brain just wouldn't cooperate. The more I attempted to swallow my fears–tell myself that nightmares couldn't hurt me and that it was all in my head–the more I thought about how that figure would harm me.

And so it went on. I couldn't keep my eyes closed for any longer than five minutes before my heart rate pounded into the back of my chest. Not long after, the sky had pinkened–the sun was about to rise and put an end to my sleepless night. My head ached, rendering me able to concentrate in school the next day.

"Jeremy, son. I love you. So it frustrates me that I have to tell you this again: it's all in your damn head."

"Stuart, please have more patience with him. Can't you see the dark circles under his eyes?"

"No, I'm at my wits end with this kid! We've already tried everything."

I reluctantly agreed to sleep on my own again that night. They were grownups, after all. They told me they'd gone through this exact thing when they were kids. They said I was exaggerating just to get their

THEM

attention. Dad stressed that I simply had to *man up*–I was apparently acting like a girl, which, to him, was shameful.

I sucked it up and did as I was told.

I crawled into bed, letting darkness envelop the room. I lay down on my side, and forced myself to take in deep, even breaths. I willed myself to relax, only to find myself in the dimly lit bathroom once again. I reached up to find the light switch but couldn't seem to reach it. I turned to the door, only for the doorknob to disappear. Someone was calling my name. My eyes snapped open from the shallow sleep, only to register that same voice from the dream. It was a whimpering tune emanating from the bathroom.

"Jeremy."

I held my breath, waiting for the thing to speak again. If it didn't, maybe I could convince myself this wasn't happening–

"Jeeeeeremyy." The voice made my heart clench up in my chest.

I rested the second pillow over my head. I lodged balls of tissue as deep into my ears as they could go. In spite of my best efforts, that same deep, simpering voice that sounded like it was echoing from the pipes drifted into my consciousness. The nightmare became so frequent I

THEM

was able to recall it with precise clarity even after I'd woken up. And each time I rose from it, the first thing I'd see was that same figure of a man–one who stood at least nine feet tall–standing in the corner by the window.

I sauntered into the bathroom to inspect it–it was empty.

"Jeremy... oh, Jeremy..."

There it was again, coming from the sink.

Every night since then, this would happen in an endless loop. The bathroom, the nightmare. That damned shadow. I thought he'd remain in that same corner for my entire life, but as the years passed, he'd come closer and closer. Sometimes I'd even see him from outside my window. Sometimes I'd wake up to see his dark, featureless head looking down at me, inches away from my face. I'd blink, and he'd be gone... and then the nightmare would begin all over again.

When I entered my final year in high school, mom told me she heard that Nadia had committed suicide. She'd slit both her wrists and plunged a knife into the center of her throat. She was thirty-three. I suppose she too had been an introvert who'd played the game. My guess now is that she made me play it because she

THEM

needed someone else to suffer alongside her. I think she couldn't stand to be the only one tormented by the sleepless nights, the waking existence of utter exhaustion, and mental depletion. Going through the day fatigued and fighting for cat naps just to rest because night time was cold and un-survivable.

Today is the eve of my thirty-third birthday. Counting down the hours to midnight fuels the burning sensation in my chest. After all these years, the voices haven't stopped. The specter still looms in the shadows, getting closer and closer to me with each passing day. I don't know what it will do when it finally reaches me, nor do I care to find out.

I curse the world for the life of constant suffering I had grown up with. I never knew how to live; I only knew how to endure.

Tonight, however, I will rest easy knowing I won't be alone in my suffering. None of the kids have class today, as it is a public holiday. Yesterday, however, I made them each play *The Mirror Game* during homeroom for extra credit. I told them it would look good on their permanent record, and that Mr. Sanders would give them a golden star for their active participation alone. Each and every one of them

THEM

obliged–they were happy to, finally, be doing something that wasn't academic. Getting a gold star for playing a game? How could a young, developing mind refuse such a fantastic wager?

I amble out of bed and open the drawer on my nightstand.

I would love to see the fruits of their suffering, but time is almost up. The clock ticks, signaling the arrival of my thirty-third birthday.

Any moment now.

The searing pain in my chest that accompanies Dylan's arrival throbs. He's near. I loaded one single bullet into the Beretta M9 I purchased last week in anticipation for today. I expected to be more nervous, though, in all honesty, the chief emotion that ebbs over me is one of relief. I hold the barrel of the gun up to my temple and count down with the clock...

Three...

Two...

One...